BUSTED

OLIVIA SINCLAIR

1

Aiden

I'm leaning back in my ancient, creaky desk chair, contemplating the multicolored stacks of files and paperwork on my desk. They represent the last hurdle of my active military career. Why did I leave all this to the last minute? It's not like I didn't know this day was coming for the last six months. I could have sorted through them in small batches every day, sending them to the archives, shredding, or setting them aside for my successor on any number of days since. But I didn't. Something more important always came up.

The reality is, I hate paperwork. So here I sit, rubbing my tired eyes, trying to decide where I should start. I've got a little less than two weeks to empty this office. The view out of the window no longer distracts me with the endless blue sky of southern California and a couple of too tall palm trees that mostly just sit there unless the wind picks up with an incoming storm.

The phone on my desk rings suddenly and shrilly. *Saved by*

the bell, I think until I glance at the caller ID and groan. It's my older sister, the one that thinks she *always* knows what I should do with my life and which one of her divorced friends I should ask out next. I did that once and let me say, never again.

I pick up the phone anyway, "Hey, Linda."

"I'm so mad right now, little brother, I could spit."

I double-check the phone. Linda's too bossy to get mad. Eileen is the sister with always simmering rage. "Linda?"

"Yes, it's me. Didn't mean to scare you A-ten."

I grit my teeth. That's the other thing I hate, being called that ridiculous nickname that should have been left behind forty years ago. I'm fucking forty-five years old. But to my siblings, I'm still the baby of the family. Fuck my life.

"Linda, I'm still at work…"

"Yes, yes, and you hate the nickname. I know. But you'll always be my baby brother. And yes, I did call for a reason so don't get your dress whites all sweaty."

I'm not wearing dress whites of course, but my family has never been particularly concerned with that level of accuracy in *anything* they do.

"So why *did* you call?"

"Well, partly it's to check in on you before you retire. I can't believe you get to retire before I do. You always get off easy. But mostly it's to complain that my favorite romance author is now dead to me and it's all your fault."

"How can that possibly be my fault?" I'm rapidly descending into ingrained sibling levels of outrage, which is not a good sign. I'm not even going to dignify her accusations of unfairness with a response because all she's doing is falling into our same old groove too. Sometimes I think she says this stuff without even realizing she's saying it. It's all become a familiar habit that she rather enjoys taking out and trying on again to see if it still fits.

"Apparently she's one of your old girlfriends and I just

found out you're the model for all her heroes. No matter how hard I tell myself it's fiction, I just can't enjoy reading about my little brother's dick."

I want to know why she's reading about anybody's dick, but that's a guaranteed rabbit hole I don't want to go down. "Linda," I sigh heavily, already feeling a headache of enormous proportions beginning to swell and throb behind my eyes, "Please start at the beginning." I'm pleading here.

"You know my absolute favorite author is Darla Simone, right?"

"No, but keep going."

"Well, she is. Or was. Anyway, I've read everything she's written, which is about twenty books now, there's a new one due in a few months. Dammit."

"Linda," I beg.

She sighs with equal impatience right back at me, "And you know Todd and I took that vacation up in the Catskills last week?"

"Yes, I remember. A romantic getaway that you told me way more than I wanted to know about before you left."

"Ha. Well, I forgot to take my phone charger and Todd refused to go back for it so I didn't have any of my ebooks available. Which meant while he was out fishing, I had to entertain myself in the cottage because it's not like there was any place to go shopping. And well, there were a bunch of old paperbacks in the living room that other people had left behind."

"Keep going. Maybe a little faster?"

"Gah, you are so impatient!" She pauses to take a long drink of something. "Anyway, one of the paperbacks was Darla's first novel, *Deal with the Devil,* which of course I've read, but it's been a few years."

"So you reread it, good for you. What does that have to do with me?"

"Everything. Yes, I reread it, but it wasn't the same book. Quite a few details had been changed. Or rather, the book I read originally — the ebook — differed from the print copy."

"Still don't see what this has to do with me."

"You know that stupid-ass tattoo you have by your dick?"

Oh, fuck. "Yes, but how do you?"

"There are a lot of things I wish I could unsee, baby brother. And you and Todd having a literal pissing contest the night before our wedding is at the top of the list."

I stand up, trailing the cord of the desk phone behind me, and I lock my office door. I may only have days left in the Navy, but this could fuel salacious rumors for years.

"There have to be other people with that tattoo, Linda. It's just coincidence."

"You sure about that? The exact number of reviews on it is listed in the book as 53,692."

My mouth is dry, "What's her name again?"

"Darla Simone, but I'm sure that's a pen name. Have you slept with any romance authors?"

"Not that I know of. But wait, you said you'd read all her books, they can't all have that tattoo?"

"No, in fact, none of the ebooks do. But when I found that, I went back and checked. They're all basically the same guy, same personality, same build, same dick described in intimate detail." She's back to sounding angry. "Hair and eye color change around a bit, but it's the same guy. And now I can't read any of them and I think you ought to sue."

"Because you're out a few books to read?"

"Yes, and because she's clearly profited from you without your knowledge."

I'm a lot less worried about that than my reputation in the private sector where I'm set to take over as Chief Medical Officer and head of surgery at Destiny Bay General Hospital in about three months.

"Did you bring the book back with you?"

"Yes. You want it, don't you?"

"I do. Can you send it to my apartment and not my office? I'm wrapping up here in the next few days."

"Okay. Seriously, I can't believe my baby brother is retiring. It makes me sound so old!"

"You'll forget about it when I go back to work. It's not like I'm going to be sitting around playing golf for the next twenty years."

"No, but Todd's hoping you'll visit and he can get a few rounds in."

"Umm, I'll see," is the best I can manage. I hate golf. Todd's generally a good guy, despite having gone into the Air Force, but I'd rather go fishing with him. "Linda? Thanks for letting me know."

"I do love you, Aiden. You know that, right? Even if you've ruined my favorite books."

"Love you too."

I look around my office again. The paperwork is going to have to wait one more day. I'm too distracted to concentrate on it, and it looks like I have some reading to do. The last thing I need is to be caught reading a smutty romance by my staff, so it's time to head home.

2

______

Aiden

I arrive back at my apartment, technically a condo that I'm renting from a buddy who was transferred abroad, dreading my upcoming reading list.

The first thing I do after setting my briefcase in its designated spot on the hallway credenza is pour myself a really stiff scotch. I glance around the place I've called home for the last five years and realize it's always felt temporary. It even smells neutral, there's nothing to distinguish it from any upscale hotel room anywhere in the country. Even the windows look out on the faces of other nondescript high-rise buildings. Now I'm wondering why I never tried to do something about that. Make the place reflect my personality with something. Buy a houseplant or a painting. Maybe because, like most military postings, I knew this was temporary and it was likely to be my last. I was ready to move on and build something a little more permanent in one location, put down some roots.

Marriage is not in the cards for me despite the many

suddenly single friends offered up to me on silver platters. *Everyone* has that single friend, and some of them are nice enough women. But most reek of desperation, and who knows what's really under that? None of it matters because not one of them is right for me.

My ex-wife was pretty close on paper, but once the ring was on her finger, not so much. But that doesn't mean I wouldn't like to see the same group of guys for poker every month or fuck a few women that can have an intelligent conversation and understand the concept of no strings. In other words, they aren't desperate and don't start talking about wedding venues and naming our kids before we've even ordered dinner. I live for my work. I don't want or need anything that tries to distract me from that priority.

I have to wait a few days for Linda to send me the hard-core evidence, but that doesn't mean I can't get started on the related research. Unfortunately, that means reading all of Ms. Simone's books.

I head into the living room and stretch out on the brown leather couch, I might as well be comfortable while I torture myself. I gulp the scotch (that's a sin) and bring up Darla Simone's search results on my phone. I shudder when I see the covers. Buff, naked men cavorting hither and yon. Okay, they're not completely naked, but there's a lot of six and eight packs trying to entice the female readership. And the titles are just as bad. Who reads this shit? Besides my sister, that is.

I go back to the basic search engine screen and type in *Darla Simone books in order*. From what Linda described, it sounds like she made more mistakes early in her career, which makes sense, most people do. It's the stupid ones that never learn from their mistakes, and as annoying as she is, my sister is extremely smart and unlikely to keep reading the works of a stupid person. So I might as well start with book number two. I'll save the first in the series for the paperback arriving in the mail. One thing I'm not doing is reading this shit anymore than necessary.

Darla Simone's second book is entitled *Devil's Promise*. I get up to pour another drink. It's going to be a long night. Back on the couch, I brace myself and start reading.

Surprisingly, by the third chapter, I'm actually almost enjoying myself. Darla's got a snarky mouth on her and she doesn't seem to take any of this too seriously. I take another sip of scotch, letting its mellow burn sit on my tongue, and put the crystal glass down on the floor within easy reach.

I'm chuckling by the time I read to where the characters start getting intimate. I pause when I hit the first love scene because the hero is six foot four and the woman is five foot two. While his cock is buried in her pussy, he's also kissing her mouth. I stop to ponder that. I'm the same height as the main character and a five foot two woman would be... I stand up and hold one hand at chest height. Standing, the top of her head would be right about where my nipples are. Adjusting for the sex they're having, which would mean the necessary equipment needs to line up, she'd be higher up than that but still not where I could kiss her. Unless of course, the hero has a spine that can make loops like a snake, or she has the shortest legs and longest torso never before seen by medical science.

I grin and go back to the story. Halfway through, I'm starting to understand what Linda was talking about. This seems to be based on me. Some of my mannerisms are in there, along with certain speech patterns, but they're more casually slipped in. This is someone that's probably met me, likely more than once, but definitely not someone I've fucked. It doesn't make sense that a former lover would observe me that closely in all other areas and then go another fictional direction in the bedroom.

I don't cum before she does. Ever. And while it's true I like to be in charge, I've never ordered a woman to suck my cock.

Now if she offers? That's a different story, and I don't recall turning anyone down. But demanding it is not my style.

I keep reading, skimming over the love scenes as I've mostly ruled them out for clues. A couple of phrases catch my eye here and there. Things that feel familiar, like I know who says them often, but I can't put my finger on it.

The book ends with — surprise — a happy ending and even more sex. I'm not too much the wiser, so I download book three. This one is *Devil's Delight*. I should really grab some dinner, but I'm too caught up in this research project to take a break. I could always order take out, but I really prefer to cook. That way I know exactly what I'm eating. I decide to keep reading, at least for a few chapters, and then I'll put it down and fix a light dinner.

It only takes a few pages to see that in theory, it's a different guy, but he's still well over six foot. This time the hero's also a doctor like me. Hmmm. Let's find out if she got that part right. That could eliminate quite a few potential suspects. Meh, not so much I realize as I'm a couple of chapters in. Definitely not anyone from work then. That's a small but sweet relief.

As the doctor chases the sweet virginal nurse down the halls (none of the nurses I've ever met would put up with that for even five seconds) I find a serious clue. The layout of this particular public hospital in San Diego is described perfectly. Right down to the way the tables are arranged in the cafeteria. The treatments and procedures are still how a non-medical person would describe them, but my new friend Darla has definitely been in that hospital.

I've never worked in the San Diego public sector. But my best friend has for about the last twenty years. I thought when I moved here I'd see him regularly, but actually, I've seen him less than when I was stationed in Washington State. It's been a couple of years since we've connected in person because work keeps getting in the way, but I do at least try to get a phone call in at least once a month. God, now I feel guilty over not making more time for him, although he's possibly busier with work than I am.

I think back to any women I might have met while visiting Tristan. His wife died six or seven years ago from sudden and severe leukemia. He has a sister I've met a few times and there were some doctors and nurses that came to a summer party he once threw when I happened to be there, a *long* time ago. He has a daughter, Rose, but she's way too young for this stuff.

A curl of dread drops into my stomach when I mentally bring up a picture of her. No. She really isn't too young. Rose would be… I do the math in my head… just about twenty-three now. I do a quick search on my phone to see the date when Darla's first book was published. Four years ago.

Fuck.

3

$$Aiden$$

Sleazy doesn't even begin to describe how I feel wondering if Rose wrote about me like that. Even considering if my best friend's daughter would ever think about me sexually appalls me.

I'm tired. I've been drinking. I haven't eaten. I'll have a much better theory in the morning to explain everything that does not involve nineteen-year-olds fantasizing about my cock. I make myself go into the kitchen and cook a simple stir-fry. It's late. I should have been in bed a few hours ago and I don't like to eat so close to bed, but a stomach filled only with scotch, even if it is the expensive stuff, will leave me tossing and turning all night.

The seed of doubt has been planted, though, and it doesn't take long to sprout. I go to bed trying to figure out if there is even a possibility that Rose ever saw me naked. I can't think of one. And Tristan is not the kind of man that would describe my privates to a teenage girl and most definitely not his own daughter. Now I'm half dreading the book on its way from my sister. Do I really want to know? No. It's more that I *have* to know. All I can hope for is there's something in there that points to another person or puts a more innocent spin on the whole thing. But the more I think about it, the less likely either scenario is.

No big surprise, I don't sleep well. I wake up gasping in the early morning, my cock throbbing. I'd been dreaming of Rose on her knees, her pretty, naturally pink lips tightly sealed around my cock. Her blue eyes smiling into mine. Fuck, I don't *want* this to be her, do I? Maybe retiring from the Navy has brought on a sudden mid-life crisis. A subconscious attempt to recapture my youth. Of course, it was Linda that called *me* out of the blue.

Midlife crisis or not, my morning hard-on is too far gone to recede without intervention. I head into the shower and try to think of anything else besides Rose while I take care of it. The last woman I slept with? Nope, can't even remember what she looked like — before I'm crucified for that it was over a year ago. The emergency room nurse I've always thought was hot? Suddenly she's not all that. In desperation, I even conjure up an image of my ex-wife, guaranteed to shrivel any erection within a six-mile radius. I'm indifferent, my cock still aching for something it knows damn well it can't have. And suddenly I'm back in my dream, other tantalizing images surfacing from my subconscious. Rose naked in my bed, her red-gold hair spread out on the sheets. Rose bent over the bathroom counter, her ass mine for the taking. Cum sprays out on the shower walls, fast and furious. "Fuck!" I shout, my anger and frustration reverberating off the granite tile.

I head into work on time and as penance for all my dirty, inappropriate thoughts, I dive right into the piles on my desk. A few hours later my assistant comes in bringing me back to the present, "Sir? Everyone is waiting in the break room. It's your goodbye lunch today. I put a reminder on your calendar."

Oh God, he did. "Sorry, Evans. Yes, you did. I'll be right there."

I hate these kinds of things, but it's never been about me. I shake hands and make small talk, wondering if the package from Linda has arrived yet. It's the same small boring sandwiches we have at every one of these get-togethers, so I give them a hard pass. The three strawberries that were added as a garnish are anemic, as is the handful of curly kale. You'd think this was all military issue, but it's not, it's just such a hassle to set up the billing for an approved vendor that whoever puts in the orders just goes with what's on file as already approved. It's easier for everyone concerned. And the staff are divided down the lines of 'will eat any and all free food' and those that prefer to do their own thing no matter what. I have a sneaking suspicion this part of the job will stay with me for the rest of my career. I'm half expecting to be greeted by the exact same sandwich tray when I arrive at my new job a thousand miles away.

When I can, I escape the hospital. While I'm technically on call for any of my patients, their routine care has already been transitioned to other doctors as have any planned surgeries. I'm mostly here to answer questions… and deal with those damn files.

There's a slim package waiting for me with my mail when I arrive back at my apartment building. I grab the pile and head to the elevator without looking through it. I'll open it when I get in my apartment, even though my stomach is churning. It's mid-afternoon and I can't remember a time when I was home this early when I wasn't sick, which isn't exactly a common occurrence. I eye the thin package like it's a coiled snake. I don't want to open it. But I need to know.

I leave the rest of the mail on the credenza. I'll deal with the day-to-day stuff later. Instead, I take the package into the living room. Linda didn't bother with a note, so I extract the paperback from the packaging and sit down on the couch. Somehow the cover looks even sillier on an actual physical book than it does on the screen. I brace my elbows on my knees and start reading.

The same snarky humor is there, only this time it's Rose's voice I hear reading the words, rolling her eyes with a little wry grin. The writing is a bit rougher than the later books, but there's something more spontaneous about it because of that. Rose has always been funny and a lot smarter than her peers.

Maybe this isn't her. I mean, where would she find the time? Going to school full-time and writing twenty some odd books? That doesn't add up. For the first time today, a sense of relief comes over me. It can't be Rose.

I go back to the *Deal with the Devil.* I read the chapter that so alarmed Linda. She's right, that's describing my tattoo, the one that was a mistake. I didn't set out to claim 53,000 people thought I was all that. I haven't had it removed because I don't need anyone messing with a laser that close to my cock. And it was the ultimate lesson in humility. Even if it's not particularly large — the tattoo, that is — my cock has never had any complaints.

I stop at the end of the chapter to make a sandwich, avocado and turkey with sun-dried tomatoes and some iced tea which I carry back into the living room. I'd love to wrap this up today, but I have a feeling it's going to blow up into something bigger than I can anticipate right now. Probably that dread still churning in my stomach is fueling my imagination. I eat my sandwich while I keep reading, looking for clues.

"Ah, fuck," I groan in dismay from somewhere in chapter eleven. It's an almost verbatim conversation I recall having with Tristan about a year after his wife died. I'd been trying to encourage him to get out of the house since Rose was heading to college soon, and he'd been adamant that he wasn't interested.

His wife had been it for him. I remember it because it was one of the few times he got angry with me. Reading it like this makes me feel like an ass, but in fairness, I've never had a relationship that ended well, so I didn't really understand where Tris was coming from. I hadn't been pushing for more than getting him to go for drinks at a local bar and look around. At least I haven't been immortalized saying something even more crass.

I think back to that conversation, surprised I can even remember it. It was in late summer. Rose had already gone to bed and Tristan and I were out on his patio drinking beer and talking about life, at least up until I tried to introduce the topic of getting back out there. Nothing exciting happened, no raised voices or anything a neighbor would likely pay attention to. But if I remember correctly, Rose's room was upstairs at the back of the house.

Fuck, I'm not going to be able to stop with this book, I'm going to have to read *all* of Darla's titles, aren't I? Find out what else I've said not knowing someone else was listening.

4

____

Rose

"It's noon, Ing!" I shout to my best friend and roommate from the weathered front door of our house. She's busy pushing an overstuffed tote bag into an already overstuffed and aging Honda.

"Almost done!" she calls back, flipping her long blonde braid to her back as she tries to shut the hatchback. It doesn't want to close, so she pushes a few more things around, making the little car shake violently.

"We did it, babe. We're officially college graduates. Leave that for a few minutes and come have a glass of champagne." We are celebrating the shit out of this day. As long as we're both safely on the road by five, that is. Which is why any alcohol needs to be consumed (in moderation) over lunch.

She laughs as she finally makes the door latch and locks the car before it can change its mind. She named her car Bob while mine is Kevin. It's an inside joke between us for lots of different reasons. The primary one is that these are the main men in our lives and it makes sense that they do not have sexy names because, well… our love lives are yeah, not.

"Come on. Pizza's getting cold." I'm impatient to eat and celebrate, not to say goodbye to my BFF for what could be years. I mean, I hope not, but neither of us really knows where the next phase in life will take us. Our favorite pizza creation, honed over the last four years of school, is waiting on the coffee table. Thankfully, we rented this place furnished. It's cheap college-style stuff, but we don't have to dispose of it or move it.

Ingrid finally comes in and goes to wash her hands in the kitchen sink, before plopping down on the floor inches from the pizza. "Hey, Rose? Thanks for waiting for me."

"Err, it's just pizza, Ing. I can manage a few minutes, really."

"No, I meant this whole year. You could have graduated last year and left me here by myself. I'd have understood, but I'm glad you stayed."

"That was as much for me as you. Now let's start the toasts. We have a lot to get through. I made a list." I'm half teasing as I pour champagne into the disposable flutes I found at a party supply store. Once the last bag of trash goes out to the curb, we're out of here. Everything is packed, including the dishes. "Let's start with a toast to Darla Simone who got us through."

"To Darla!" Ingrid raises her glass with a bright smile. She takes a sip and then raises the flute again, "To letting go of pointless crushes."

We're both grimacing a little at that one but dutifully drink. Part of what brought us together all those years ago in the worst creative writing class ever was our shared experience lusting after older men who barely acknowledged our existence. And we both agreed it was better that they didn't, really. Knowing that doesn't make it less painful though, or letting go any easier. We've decided that graduation means it's time to put away childish things. Like crushes on men who don't want us back and secrets. Well, all except one.

It's also time I told my dad I've already got a serious income and that his mortgage is now paid off. I have to get that last part out before he gets the official letter in about a week. But nobody needs to know that it's my words behind the wildly popular books of Darla Simone. Only Ing knows that little detail, and she'll never breathe a word. I made a few mistakes early on. After all, I didn't set out to be a smutty romance author, it sort of just happened. I learned fast though and got my act together. I'm pretty solidly established in that career now, I think. And the majority of my readers are raving fans that keep begging for more.

But there's one critical part of Darla's world I need to change. I've agreed with Ing that it's time to stop using my long-standing crush as my primary inspiration. Readers are starting to complain that they've seen the characters before in previous books and that the sex scenes are getting a bit monotonous. I'm sorry, okay? There's only so much I can imagine with no real experience. I do a lot of reading though, all in the name of research.

Ing has been acting as my assistant and media consultant ever since Darla's sales took off. That's another reason I went for the five-year graduation plan so we could keep working together in the same location. Yeah, I could have graduated and gotten an apartment nearby, but then I would have had to explain everything to Dad and well, this last year has been really good to me financially. And Ing too, of course. I've been able to pay her well, and she's socked it all away for her independent life, which starts in just a few hours.

Ingrid is an heiress, an orphaned one with a trust fund she can't access until she's thirty-five. She also has a stern guardian (the object of her crush, of course). He's ordered her back to New York to live in his fabulous penthouse and work in his law firm as some kind of general assistant (since she doesn't have any kind of law degree). She has a degree in marketing as of today, which is why she was such a big part of Darla's success.

There are so many problems with Justin's plans for her. For starters, he yells. A lot. Ing doesn't do well with people that shout. I'd have told him off years ago, but she just gets quieter and quieter until she can find a dark corner and cry for a week. Her guardian never seems to catch on or he doesn't care. We can never decide which. The other big problem is that his lover stays over frequently. It's almost guaranteed if Ingrid and Justin manage to have a civil conversation (once in a blue moon) Margot will saunter out of his bedroom the next morning. Now I'm not judging a grown man and what he does in privacy, but when a young woman living there is in love with you? Total salt in the wound. Nobody should be surprised she doesn't want to go back to that.

And it's not lost on either of us that this sounds like a modern version of a Regency romance novel. For five seconds, I considered writing it up and giving Ing a fictional happy ending to cheer her up about the whole thing. But I'm at least smart enough not to include a prominent attorney in my fictional world where he could easily be identified and sue my pants off.

Anyway, that's why Ingrid has come with me on most vacations and holidays. Dad thinks of her as a second daughter by now, I swear. And it's why we're in a hurry to get out of here. Dad readily accepted my excuse for skipping graduation as all my other friends graduated last year, so what was the point? I told him we could do dinner when I came to visit, which is where I'm headed.

But Justin wouldn't hear of it when Ingrid presented a similar argument. Of course he never really listens when Ing tries to stick up for herself. And to make it worse, he managed to get Margot in as one of the commencement speakers. She's some kind of muckety-muck in finance, but really she's the last straw.

So we both skipped the ceremony to pack and, well, run away. Ing is going to go on a slow road trip across the south before ending up on the North Carolina coast, where she's rented a small cottage for six months. She's going to make some stops at places she's always wanted to see and then hole up to work on her jewelry designs. She's got a new cell phone under my company name, *Rosey Red Publishing*. The one Justin pays for will be left on the kitchen counter for when he tries to trace her. Which will probably be about fifteen minutes after she doesn't show up for the dinner he ordered her to attend. It's all a highly dramatic plan to basically cut him off completely, but I'm guessing Ing will let him back in her life when she finally meets someone else.

I'd half like to stick around to see his face when he comes looking for her, but the one time I met him I could tell he wasn't impressed with me so best to leave that one alone. Maybe someday I'll make him an alpha-hole hero since he's the real-life prototype. Right now I couldn't do that to Ing, plus there's the whole lawsuit thing.

She swears he has a softer side, but I think it's her imagination. We've agreed to disagree and to leave all that emotional turmoil behind when we drive off independently into the sunset.

We're grown-ups now. Or at least we should try to act like it.

5

Rose

And what silliness am I leaving behind? I've had a crush on my dad's best friend Aiden McBride since, well… for as long as I can remember. When my mom got sick, I think I adopted him as a fun fantasy to disappear into when the real world kept getting suckier. It was a completely safe dream because I knew it was never, ever going to happen.

Aiden is a good guy. He's a top surgeon in the Navy and has never once even glanced at me inappropriately. He's stern and gorgeous. I swear all he does is sleep, cut people open, and workout because that's the only thing that can explain those abs.

And no, he's never paraded around in front of me half-naked, sadly. It's just when he visits Dad and stays overnight, he usually bunks in the tiny guest house in the back garden. The guest house I can see into from my bedroom window.

I know, I know. Adult me says you shouldn't invade some-one's privacy like that. Sixteen-year-old me had a slightly different moral code. And I hate to admit this, but she's still not sorry she looked. He's *beautiful.*

It's time to come out of the cave I've stuffed myself into though, the one where I'm all alone. Aiden's not for me. He's never brought a girlfriend with him when he visits. Heck, he never brought his wife around when he was married. His divorce helped fuel my fantasies, of course. I was totally up for comforting him! Thank God I never actually offered that.

I usually disappear when he comes to visit. He's there to see Dad, and I'd rather watch him from afar when I don't have to worry about being caught doing it. I'm positive he has no idea I've been having dirty thoughts about him all these years. He'd be mortified. I'd be mortified. Dad would well, let's not go there. Nobody needs to know.

I don't imagine I'll be seeing him anymore anyway, now that I'm out of school. I haven't quite decided where I'm going to live, but it won't be in San Diego. If I were smart, I'd move out of California and go somewhere with a lower cost of living. But Dad's my only family, and I'd at least like to be close enough to drive to see him in a day. I'm toying with some of the smaller towns between San Francisco and the Oregon border. Heck, maybe I'll even look around in Oregon. There's always Las Vegas, but I don't really see myself and Sin City being that great a match. I'll figure it out in a few months. I've got time.

Right now though, I've got a deadline for my next book. I have to get at least the first draft done in thirty days, and I haven't even started. So I'm planning to spend a few days with my dad and grab the keys to our mountain cabin. I'm going to go up there since there won't be any distractions, and I'll write the damn thing.

It's causing quite a bit of stress because for the first time I'm not self-publishing, so a lot of people are going to be mad if I don't make my commitment. And Ing and I agreed this book wouldn't star Aiden (again) as the hero. It has to be someone completely different. That's part of my problem with getting started. I'm not actually sure I can do that. I still don't see myself as a real author, I've just been writing new fantasies that I dream up about Aiden.

That creative writing professor certainly never thought I was a real writer. She'd asked for an essay on our first broken heart. I'd never had one because I'd never been in love (we're not really counting Aiden here, I seriously had zero expectations from him). But what college sophomore is going to admit to that? So I dove deep into my diary full of wild fantasies and was publically ridiculed in front of the class by the professor. It was humiliating.

But Ing was there, and it was how we became friends. She came up to me later, gave me a hug, and told me all about her yearning for her older guardian. She's the one that eventually suggested turning it all into a full-length romance. It was mostly a fun way to spend Friday nights since neither of us were into parties. I just kept spinning the tale longer and longer (and crazier). When it was done, we figured out how to self publish it. It sold five thousand copies in the first week, and Darla Simone was born.

I dropped out of the creative writing class after the 'incident' and then I cut back on my class schedule the next semester to write more. I was tempted to reveal my success to that miserable professor, but having read her one and only attempt at popular fiction, I knew it would fall on deaf ears. I'm pretty sure she's of the opinion that a happy-ever-after is the equivalent of selling out. I'm content watching the size of deposits grow in my account.

But a few months ago I agreed to the offer of a small publisher in part to see what they could do for me that I couldn't do for myself but really to give Ing a break. Publishing is not her dream and while we've propped each other up, she deserves time to explore her own career. She knows I'll be here with open arms if it doesn't work out, or if she just needs a steady income while she figures things out. But for the next six months, she's no longer Darla's right hand.

Ing and I eat our fill of the mushroom, spinach, olive, and feta pizza and drink all the champagne. It was a small bottle, so that's not saying too much. It's not a huge celebration, but we had to do something to mark the occasion.

There's still a few slices of pizza left and I wrap them up in foil for Ing. I'll be at Dad's tomorrow, but she's going to be on the road for at least the next two weeks. We tidy up from lunch and then do one last check through the small house. We've lived here for the last two years. I could have afforded something fancier but fancy brings questions, so we've co-existed with other students renting nearby. Just where they had eight people in the same size house, ours held just the two of us.

I'm tearing up a little as we finish going through the empty rooms. Then Ing plops her Justin-provided phone on the kitchen counter along with a note, *I'm fine, I'm an adult. I'll be in touch when I think you won't yell. Love, Ingrid*

I raise an eyebrow at the 'love' part, but Ing shrugs and pulls out her new phone. She's had it for about a month to make sure everything's transferred and ready to go.

"You've got my dad's number in there too, right? Just in case?"

"Yes. Right here, see Rose and then Rose's Dad."

"I guess this is it then?" I'm sniffing a bit. It's been a good few years. Maybe not the normal college experience, but I have most definitely learned a lot.

"Cheer up, Rose. Darla has work to do. Go out and find some inspiration!"

"Yeah, guess I'd better hit the bars in Coronado. Find a nice Navy SEAL to *inspire* me." I wiggle my eyebrows suggestively.

"You go, girl."

We both know I'll do no such thing, although if I don't get this book started soon I may have to do something equally drastic. I'm still not sure Justin isn't going to find Ingrid and drag her home within the week. The man has private investigators on his regular payroll. Why wouldn't he use them? But Ing thinks he doesn't really want her there, that he's just going through the motions out of a sense of duty. She says he won't waste time finding her if she's not on his immediate to-do list.

There's still a couple of hours before our self-imposed five o'clock deadline, but there's also no point in lingering. Ing will feel better when she puts a few more miles between her and Justin, and I'd like to get closer to San Diego before I stop for the night. So we lock up and put the keys under the flowerpot as agreed with the landlord and head out. I follow Ing to the freeway and then honk and wave as she takes the eastbound on-ramp. I move over into the left lane to turn west.

6

Rose

I drive for three or four hours before deciding it's time to get off the freeway and find a room for the night. It's been an emotional day and there's still a ways to go tomorrow so no point in pushing it right now. There's a decent-looking hotel that's part of a chain not too far from the exit. I'm grateful I don't really have to worry about the price, not that it's expensive, but if I had been a traditional college student with no job under my belt, it might be.

My dinner options are less exciting. I've seen enough of the inside of my car for a while. The last thing I want to do is more driving to find something more interesting than the fast-food options by the exit, and there may not be any, regardless. I'm not sure this is even a town. It has all the hallmarks of a wide spot in the road. So I go with tacos from a drive-up window and take them back to my room.

Curling up on the bed with the TV remote in one hand, I take a big crunchy bite out of the end of one taco, slurping up the escaping beef and cheese with my tongue. Not bad for dinner in a bag. There is of course nothing to watch. The hotel has the basic cable package, but nothing is the least bit interesting. I don't know why I bother flipping through channels, except I'm feeling restless. In a lot of ways, I'm excited to get on with my life. But I'm dreading the next month of writing. And then there's telling my dad I've been basically lying to him for the last two years when I told him I'd gotten a scholarship so he didn't have to pay my tuition.

My dad's a pediatrician in a hospital so he makes decent money, but my mom's medical bills were outrageous even with insurance. Then my dad's soft heart and the cost of living in San Diego sucks out the rest. He donates a lot to all the kids' charities that end up paying his salary, so sometimes I wonder why he doesn't just work for free. It would cut down on the paperwork, at least in my simplistic view of the world. I was so relieved not to be a burden on him anymore. I know he would never see it that way, but I like my independence. And I value knowing that if something comes up in my life, I can handle it myself.

I miss Ing already. It's probably too soon to text. I know she was hoping to put at least five hundred miles between her and Justin tonight. I roll my eyes at the thought of her drama-filled gothic romance. At least that's what it is in her head. I'm not sure what goes on in Justin's. And I don't really see how they could ever have a future together.

After clicking through channels continuously for ten minutes, which is a lot like standing in front of an open refrig-erator hoping something new will magically appear, I finally settle on a nature special featuring seaweed. It's *almost* as exciting as my life, and I let the soothing sound of divers' air bubbles wash over me as I polish off my tacos. Then I grate-fully turn off the TV and the lights and go to bed. I now know more about underwater vegetation than I ever thought I would — and sort of wish I didn't.

In the morning, I take my time getting showered and dressed. I'm not exactly in a rush, but this hotel room is not really a place that begs you to linger. It's weird not having a regular schedule.

Even though I'm not settled in a home of my own, I know I only have one deadline and that doesn't have much to do with whether I get up at seven or ten.

There's a free (and you can tell why) breakfast buffet in the hotel lobby that I visit before I check out. I'm really hoping for better coffee and something to tide me over until I need a break from driving. But there is no coffee pot, and a quick glance tells me I'll get travel indigestion if I eat any of the hot food on offer. So I grab two bananas and a cup of yogurt and take that back to my room. I eat one of the bananas and the yogurt while I pack up and double-check that I haven't forgotten anything. Ten minutes later, I'm back on the freeway. Next stop, home.

I really need to pee. But I'm so close to my childhood home, I don't want to delay by stopping. I'll go when I get there. I make the last turn and admire all the neighbors' yards. Several people are out tidying up their flower beds and soaking up the late Spring sunshine. It's almost June now and the last time I was home was Christmas, so it's nice to see all the flowers blooming and everything looking happy. It's already warm, not hot by any means, but it will be in a few weeks.

Finally, I arrive at the end of the block and pull into our driveway. There's a black truck with tinted windows behind my dad's newer Subaru. That car suits my dad to a T and he will probably drive it for thirty years, only looking perplexed at anyone that suggests he might want to consider a newer model. He gets attached to things and people like that. It's one of the many reasons we're close.

But I've never seen that truck before, and he didn't mention expecting any visitors when I talked to him last weekend. Maybe it belongs to a contractor. Dad's been talking for years about redoing the backyard to make it more usable throughout the year.

I grab my duffle that I've packed for the next few days, my backpack, and my purse and head in. The front door is unlocked. Despite my many warnings to Dad about security, it usually is. When I step into the entry I shout, "Dad, I'm home!"

"Rose? We're on the patio." I hear faintly.

"Bathroom. Be there in a sec." I call back louder. I drop my bags in the hall and hit the half-bath that's tucked below the stairs. Everything in the house is exactly the way it was at Christmas, well minus the decorations, and the trip I made home last summer too. There's some comfort in that, but I wonder if Dad will ever think to update anything. Maybe I need to offer a makeover in a year or two?

Sighing with the relief of a now-empty bladder, I move my bags out of the way in the hallway and head to the back patio. It's a lovely space that was built right about when my mom got sick. Dad hasn't done too much with it. Not nearly what they'd planned to do together. But it's still relaxing with a table and really comfortable chairs. I hate those little wrought iron things that look really pretty but leave flower-shaped dents in your ass.

My forward momentum comes to an abrupt halt at the sliding glass doors because there, lounging with a beer next to my Dad, is Aiden. The very guy I'm supposed to not think about ever again. And he looks hotter than ever.

He's a few years younger than Dad; they met in medical school, but Dad got a later start. They look nothing alike.

Dad is well, Dad. He looks like a typical doctor, a little stooped, in his mid-fifties with dark hair and glasses. He has a kind face and a bit of a dad bod. He goes to the gym, but it's mostly because he occasionally scares himself reading cardiovascular journals.

Aiden went into the military after college and I think he does a thousand situps before he even has a cup of coffee in the morning. And while there's nothing mean about him, I wouldn't really call him kind. Stern and sexy, definitely.

He's taller than Dad, about six-four I think, and has dark hair that still doesn't have even a hint of silver in it. When I was feeling extra snarky one time I asked him if he dyed it and the perplexed look on his face was priceless. He has these blue eyes that aren't typical blue at all, and I can never pinpoint why. They always seem to reflect what he's wearing. So if he has a black shirt on they look sapphire blue, a white shirt and they're pale ice blue, but if he wears green, then they turn to teal. How can eyes do that? And give me some credit, at least I never asked him that.

Naturally, Aiden's looking at me since I just appeared in his line of sight. But there's something different, something assessing in his gaze that has me on edge.

Dad gets up and gives me a hug, "Rose! Did you have a safe trip? Sit down. Do you want a beer?"

"Yes, and no. I'm good, Dad. If I have a beer now, I'll fall asleep."

Dad pulls back just enough to look me over with a proud smile and then drops a kiss on the top of my head.

"Hey, Rose?" Aiden calls to me, dragging my attention away. He tosses something my way and I grab it instinctively — a set of car keys. "Before you sit down, there's a present for you in my truck. Top of my overnight case."

"Oh?" I do like presents and Aiden gives good ones on the

few occasions he's given me one, nothing big or fancy but always thoughtful. "Do you want me to bring your bag in?"

"No, that's okay. I'll bring it around later. No need to drag it through the house." So he's staying here then and presumably in the back guest room, which is really a glorified shed in the garden. Well, I was only planning to stay for a few days myself so I can probably cut that back to overnight, particularly if Dad has company so he won't feel lonely at my quick departure.

I head back out to the driveway, curious to see what Aiden got me.

7

———————

Rose

I'm curious to see inside Aiden's big black truck. I'm sure it's neat. He's not the type to have old hamburger wrappers in the footwell. There *might* be one or two of those in Kevin, but I'll never tell. It goes without saying that any vehicle belonging to Commander McBride will not have a name, cutesy or otherwise.

There's no cap on the back of his truck, so his bag must be either on the passenger side or behind the seats. After finding the right button to unlock the cab, I find his leather carry-on easily enough in the footwell of the passenger side. It's not big, so I can open the top flap without moving it out. Right on top is a small gift-wrapped rectangular box. The paper is the sort a fancy store would use, and there's a thin gold ribbon decorating it. I hope it's not jewelry, that would be awkward. But he's never given me anything even remotely inappropriate, so I can't imagine he would start now.

Although...

When I take the box out of his bag, I see it was carefully positioned on top of a paperback book. A book I'm *very* familiar with. Because I wrote it. Or rather, Darla did. Dread curls in my stomach and I reach for the book like a viper is going to jump out of the bag and attack my hand. I have a really bad feeling. One that's proved on point when I check the print date on the inside back cover. Fuck. I can feel all the blood draining out of my head to pool in my stomach. If I had any kind of life, it would flash in front of my eyes right now.

This is one of only two copies of *Deal with the Devil* printed with my naive newbie mistakes. I fixed the manuscript as soon as I realized there was a problem and all the ebooks have been automatically updated. Two physical copies were ordered and printed before I realized what I had done and one of them was in the UK. How on earth did Aiden end up with this one? Unless someone recognized the mistakes and sent it to him.

I eye my old red car parked out on the street. I could just run away now and change my identity. But that would take time, and I have a deadline. And then there's Dad, I can't just abandon him.

Plus, I feel a teensy bit guilty. If I were in Aiden's shoes, I would have questions. I suppose the adult thing to do is give him answers. Face the music and all that. Somehow it would be easier if I wasn't half in love with him. There's no getting out of this without looking like an idiot. Not exactly how I want the man of my dreams regarding me, even if he won't ever love me. Now he's going to look at me with disdain if I'm lucky.

At least if he wanted to humiliate me, he'd have said something in front of Dad, right? Or maybe he's not entirely sure it's me, but he's guessing? A tiny ray of hope springs to life, amongst the spaghetti of dread only to be dashed when I look down at the book and see there's a slip of paper marking a page. I open the pages like it's Pandora's box. Thank God it's not the page with the tattoo, no he's marked one with a conversation. I scan it, it's been over four years since I wrote this one and I don't remember it all that well. I'm guessing he remembers this conversation and that led him to me. But nobody else would have, so there's more to this story since I don't think he's suddenly taken to reading steamy romance.

I carefully check the book to see if he's left me any threatening messages, but there's nothing, no words on the bookmark either. I frown, wondering what to do, and finally put the book back as I found it and close the bag. I walk slowly and as calmly as I can manage back into the house carrying my present, wondering if I can bluff my way out of this. Or even if I should try.

I see there's no point in attempting that when I sit down on the patio. Dad is inside getting drinks and snacks, but Aiden's stare has hardened. His eyes are now the color of a very stormy ocean. There are harsh grooves down the side of his mouth and his chin, which could give Cary Grant a run for his money, looks sharp enough to slice cheese. He glances once into the house and then turns to me, "I expect some honest answers, Rose."

I nod, resigned.

"Midnight, at the back bench."

"Isn't that a bit melodramatic? What's wrong with after dinner?"

His lips quirk in what could almost be described as a smirk, "Clearly, I've been out of the loop on quite a bit of fucking drama. Might as well make up for lost... opportunities. On my timeline. And I think it's best if we don't have any interruptions, don't you?"

I gulp, I've no idea how to interpret that. I hold up the box, "Should I open this now?"

He shrugs lightly, "Sure, no nasty surprises there." That was a dig, I'm sure of it.

I unwrap the box carefully as Dad comes back with olives

and French bread, handing me a glass of white wine. I set it down on the glass table to take the lid off the box. It's a beautiful and elegant fountain pen. More slender than most, it's also a perfect shade of bluey-lavender enamel, my favorite color.

"It's beautiful, Aiden. Thank you."

"You're welcome." His tone is even and gives me no indications of anything. Fuck, what does he want from me? I know he doesn't want *that.* So revenge or retribution of some sort?

8

Aiden

When Tristan first told me Rose was coming home after graduation, I thought it was inspired to have it out with her at the scene of the crime, so to speak.

But now, seeing her so close knowing something of how she views me, I'm having a hard time keeping it all to myself. I want to yell. I want to kiss her. I want to shake her for making me want that. And I want to roar off in my truck and get stinking drunk. I don't do any of them because nothing on that list will solve my problems.

Rose is holding herself together fairly well after the little bombshell I left for her to find. I'm proud of her for that. She's not crying or running away. I have a bad feeling the yelling part of our conversation isn't going to be nearly as satisfying for me as I'd hoped.

And if anything, Rose is more beautiful than the last time I saw her. I can't quite put my finger on what it is, she's just more herself, I guess. If she's wearing makeup, I certainly can't tell, and there's just something about her that says she knows who she is and is content with herself. Right this minute she's exuding unconscious sex appeal. Her red-gold hair is tied back in a loose tail, and light freckles dance across her cheeks. She's fresh and natural and not trying to flirt or call attention to herself. Her lips are a perfect bow even when she's smiling wide and they're plump and pink. In other words, utterly kissable. Those damn dreams I've been having come flooding back and I shift uncomfortably in my seat. I need to deal with this situation and move on to safer territory.

Rose is also fidgeting, but in her case, I think it's pure anxiety. I've been a commanding officer long enough to know the power of letting someone sweat in their own imagination. Most of the time, that's worse than any punishment. I wonder what she thinks I'm prepared to do to her.

Rose

After that rather uncomfortable reunion on the patio, I take my bags up to my old room at the back of the house. It overlooks the backyard, but both Dad and Aiden have gone inside too. Everything is how I left it when I went away to college. Every time I come home, I throw out a few more things. I keep trying to reduce the clutter my poor Dad has to dust and vacuum. It's getting close to being an impersonal guest room, but it's not completely there yet.

The first thing I do after dumping my bags on the bed is lower the blinds and shut the curtains over them. I don't want to be tempted to (or accused of) spying on Aiden in the guest house inappropriately. Then I take a shower, pulling an old worn gypsy dress out of my closet to wear. I should get rid of it because this dress has definitely seen better days, but it was always one of my favorites, so I drag it out when I come home to wear around the house. It's loose and bohemian with about twenty different prints in all colors of the rainbow. I always feel like a social butterfly when I wear it, ready to flit around a party.

I sit down on the bed and make a list in one of the notebooks I brought with me. Often these things go in my phone or on the computer, but when I really need to think, nothing quite beats pen and paper. I resist trying out the pen Aiden got me. For starters, I'd rather wait to put ink in it until I'm settled somewhere, and second I don't really need any more reminders of him at the moment, he's already occupying items one through four on my list.

It feels like absolutely no time has passed, I'm certainly no closer to a solution to my problems when Dad calls up the stairs, "Rosey! Dinner!"

I shut the notebook and head down. It's such a familiar ritual, and yet some part of me knows it's probably one of the last times we'll go through it. Not that I won't come back to visit, but somehow when you get a permanent place of your own, everything changes. And if I have my way, it's going to include a couple of cats and a dog, maybe even some chickens if I can manage it. All that will make visiting more of a visit and less of a homecoming.

I give Dad's slightly pudgy middle a tight squeeze as I come up behind him in the kitchen.

"Oooph, where'd you get all that muscle, kid?" He teases me. "It's good to have you back, Rosey."

"Thanks, Dad. What's for dinner?"

"Nothing fancy. You know what a picky eater Aiden is. (He's not really, but he frowns a lot when there's more cheese than vegetables on the table.) So I thought we'd do tacos."

"Good plan, Dad." I don't want to tell him I had tacos for

dinner last night. Besides, Dad's are much better than any takeout joint.

He grins, "I thought so."

"What is?" Aiden wanders in from the outside patio. I'm assuming he was settling into the guest cottage.

"Tacos for dinner," I tell him, attempting to keep my voice light and natural.

"So Tris can pretend he's not loading up on cheese and refried beans?"

"Exactly." Dad and I say in unison and even Aiden's lips twitch with amusement.

Dinner is light and relaxing. If anyone else picks up on the underlying tension, nobody mentions it. It's probably just me. Aiden talks about his new job and what he's looking for in a house and Dad gets excited about some fancy imaging equipment the hospital just installed. That and the arrival of a new soft-serve ice cream machine in the cafeteria.

"Dad, you do realize you sound equally excited about both."

He pauses mid-bite of his taco and looks thoughtful, "There's already a three-week waiting list for the scanner. I only had to wait for five minutes to get a chocolate cone yesterday."

I'm careful not to look over at Aiden because I can guess he's rolling his eyes.

After dinner, I help Dad clean up and then escape to my room. I want nothing more than to crawl under the covers and get this day over with, but apparently, I'm due for more torture in… I check my phone… fuck, five and half more hours. I can hear Dad and Aiden talking on the patio over more beers. It sounds like they're discussing taking a fishing vacation. Dad's hesitating, probably because he thinks spending the money would be frivolous. Maybe he'll go when I tell him I've paid off the mortgage. I'm half-dreading that conversation because something tells me he'll think I should have invested the money instead.

To cheer myself up I text Ing with a simple,

> You busy?

but my phone rings almost instantly.

"Hey, Ing! How are you? Where are you?"

She laughs, sounding lighter than I've heard her in a few years, "Somewhere in Oklahoma I think? I found a cute little motel by the edge of the road. And get this, there's a diner across the street that serves real biscuits and gravy. My arteries are already clogged, but my heart is happy."

"Any word from Justin?"

"Not on my end, but then unless he ambushes me, how would I? And I don't think he's going to bother, Rose."

Laughter drifts up from the patio and I realize I can't have this conversation in my room. I probably shouldn't be having it at all. I walk down the hall to my dad's bedroom, the farthest from the backyard, lock the door, and go into the farthest corner — as far away from the backyard and any open windows as I can get.

"So, Ing? The Commander found out." That's how we started referring to Aiden after I showed her a picture of him in his dress uniform. Somehow we started thinking that not using his name would avoid summoning exactly what's about to happen.

She gasps, "How?"

"I don't know yet, but someone gave him one of those two paperbacks, you remember?"

"What are the odds of that? Is he mad?"

"I'm not sure. He's not breathing flames. He wants to talk later tonight. I don't think it's going to be pleasant."

"Do you need me to come? I can turn around and be there in a few days."

"No. Don't do that. I'll survive this, somehow. And I still have that deadline to deal with."

"Okay, well I'll call you tomorrow, okay? Maybe… any chance he's into you now?"

I snort at that one, "No. The vibe is disappointed uncle. I don't think there are any fun spankings on my horizon."

"Hmmm. Okay. Good luck."

We hang up and I return to my room. I might as well get a nap in, so I set the alarm on my phone and lie down on the twin bed I slept in for most of my childhood. I drift into my favorite daydream, the one where I have this perfect little house, fans who adore everything I write, a man who loves me, and everything is good.

9

Rose

My alarm goes off at 11:45 with an irritating tune. No matter how hard I look, I've yet to find one that both wakes me up and is pleasing to the ear. Anyway, I'm awake now. There's no moon, so it's really dark outside when I peel back the corner of the blind to check. There's a single light on in the back cottage, so I guess that means Aiden is still planning on talking. Not like I thought he'd change his mind.

I grab an old sweatshirt of Dad's that I keep in a drawer for just these sorts of occasions. Not the angry grilling by hot older men, but late nights sitting in the garden. There was a lot of that after my mom died. Nights when the house seemed suffocating, but getting outside helped… a little.

There's no point in turning on lights, I know how to sneak out of the house without Dad knowing. I have to avoid the squeaky third step, but that's about it. It might be harder if he believed in security systems. I slip out the sliding patio door, closing it most of the way behind me. A small gap makes it easier to open on the return trip.

I wonder how long this inquisition is going to take? There's not really that much to my side of the story.

The garden is eerie at this time of night, there's enough light from the surrounding street lights and houses to make the stone path barely visible. The white flowers sort of glow in the murk and the sweet heavy odor of jasmine is everywhere. There's an old wooden bench under the orange tree at the back. I'm pretty sure that's what Aiden was referring to.

And I was right because he's already lounging there, angled into the corner, his long legs stretched out in front of him. He's positioned so his face is in the shadows. Why do I think that was intentional?

"Hi," I say softly, stepping over his legs.

He draws them in slightly. "Rose. Take a seat."

I roll my eyes even if he can't see me. We're not in a freakin' office, for fuck's sake. I sigh as I sit down and draw my knees up under the sweatshirt. "So what do you want to know?" I'm braced for the embarrassment of revealing the depth of my crush to the one person who can tell me how pointless it is, with surgical precision. But I don't see the need to volunteer more than he wants to hear.

"Everything," he responds dryly. "But let's start with how I came to star in my friend Darla's first novel."

"You never struck me as a romance-reader type."

"I'm not. Stop trying to change the subject." His tone is dry, laced with amusement. Fuck.

"Right, well. It all started with a creative writing class. The professor was really mean. There was an assignment to write an essay about our first broken heart. But I'd never had a boyfriend or even been in love." God, I sound like such a loser, whining about my love life. I'm staring into the darkness, wondering if there's even a chance of a sinkhole opening up to save me from the worst of the embarrassment or at least put me out of my misery.

"Go on." Aiden is not going to let me off lightly. I hadn't really expected less of the Commander.

"So I dragged out my old diaries and wrote about a crush. I, um, embellished a lot. The professor read it aloud and basically called me a liar *and* a bad writer. Told me I should drop the class and sign up for economics."

Aiden says nothing. Maybe that's a good sign. Maybe if I confess all my sins this can be over and done with? "Anyway, I dropped the class, but not before I made a new friend who understood and was... well, she has her own story. Anyway, I kept adding to the plot for our own amusement until eventually, I had something book-length. I didn't write it with the intention to publish it. But my friend had a friend whose mom was an indie author. So we got this not-so-bright idea that we could package it up and maybe make enough money to you know, go to the movies, or get dinner out on Friday nights."

"And it didn't occur to you what you'd actually said in the damn thing?"

"Yes, and no." I sigh with regret. "I didn't know that some of the details were identifiable. It was only after people started leaving comments that I found out nobody else has that tattoo. Or at least it's unusual enough to be um..."

"Quite. Back up for a second and tell me how you even know about it. Because I'm pretty sure I've never paraded around here naked."

"Um, no. No, you haven't. But you tend to leave the windows open and the blinds up and well... my bedroom window looks down and um..."

"Fuck!" He keeps the volume low, but the leashed anger frightens me. I hug my knees tighter against my chest.

"What do you want from me?" I ask as calmly as I can, but cringing inside. "I changed the book as soon as I figured out there was a problem. There were only two print copies that I couldn't do anything about. A public apology would only make it worse."

"But you've kept using me, haven't you?"

"Um, well, only as inspiration. I swear I haven't invaded your privacy since I left for school."

"Really? You don't think writing characters that are clearly based on me isn't invasive?"

"But they aren't. They're based on an idea of you but not the real you."

"You've got that right." He's muttering, and I don't think he's in full agreement with my argument. "It has to stop, Rose. Now."

"I know. I'm switching everything up with this next book."

"I want to see it."

"Okay, but I haven't written it yet. I'm going to go up to Dad's cabin and get it done."

He snorts in disbelief. "I'm headed up to the cabin tomorrow. What exactly have you been planning?"

"Writing. For fuck's sake, Aiden. Did you think I was headed there to seduce you? Or spy on you? I didn't know you were here. I didn't actually talk to Dad about it yet. I thought we'd catch up for a day or two and then I'd head up for the rest of the month."

"Maybe it's a good idea. I can keep an eye on you. I don't think I'm done talking about this just yet. And I'm not sure if it's in your best interest to let you off scot-free. I need to think about it."

Fuck. I do not need an angry Navy officer hanging over my head right now. Never, really, but especially not right now.

He groans suddenly, "And don't tell your dad you're going to the cabin. He's got enough to worry about. Tell him you're off to visit a friend at the beach and I'll expect you up there in two days. Got it?"

"What does Dad have to worry about?"

"Rose."

"Fine, I'll be at the cabin in two days. Why won't you tell me about Dad?"

"Maybe because I don't go blabbing other people's business?" Sarcasm is not his best feature. "Go to bed, Rose. We'll continue this conversation when you arrive there."

Aiden

I've never been one to avoid a difficult conversation. But I let Rose circle the elephant in the room, and I didn't even try to push her on it. What the fuck?

And now I'm watching her slim form drift back towards the house. Even in the oversized sweatshirt, she's dainty compared to me. I'm not ready for bed yet. My mind is busy turning over why I didn't ask her if she still had a crush on me.

Maybe I didn't ask because it was completely inappropriate, or maybe it was because I didn't want to hear the answer like an adolescent boy asking a girl if she likes him. Because really, whether the answer is yes or no, what am I going to do about it? Absolutely nothing.

I smile without humor, wondering if Rose is going to turn on a light inside. I'm curious to see exactly how far into the tiny cottage she could see, and whether I can tell from here. But her window remains dark and eventually, I head back inside, dreading what I've just brought on myself.

In the morning I have a simple breakfast with Tris. I'm not shocked that Rose doesn't make an appearance. There's no sign of masochism in any of her books. I hate keeping secrets from my buddy, but I can't see how knowing any of this would make his life better or simpler.

He gets up and comes back with a set of keys, "You remember how to get there?"

"No," I grin, "but I remember the address and Google gave me adequate directions."

"If you're sure. Call me if you hit a snag and let me know if there are any repairs needed. I haven't been up in a while. Seems lonely without Monica or Rose."

"Sure thing." I won't do it. I'll check for issues, but I'll fix them myself or get someone else in while I'm there. Tris is doing me a favor and not charging any rent. This is the least I can do.

"Do you think Rose looked alright?" Tristan asks quietly.

"Yeah, I guess? Why?"

"I'm not sure. She seemed a little anxious. And then there's this whole five-year college thing, but she still hasn't told me what her career plans are. I guess I'm a little worried about her — not that she has to be out working an office job this week, but if she's feeling lost because her mom's not here..."

"I wouldn't worry about it, Tris. If she's still lying around on her ass at the end of the summer call me and I'll shout at her like a new recruit. Makes them jump every time."

He grins, "Deal. You're right, I shouldn't worry. Rose has never been lazy."

"Alright, I'd better hit the road. You'd better plan to come visit me up north when I get settled."

Tris nods agreeably and I head out to my truck. I already brought my bag around before breakfast. I eye Rose's ancient little car, wondering how she'll ever make it up the mountain in that thing. Or will she blow me off and run off to the beach? Am I hoping she will?

10

———

Rose

I'm a total coward. I waited until I heard Aiden's truck growl to life and pull out of the driveway before I came downstairs. By then, Dad was already gathering his briefcase and looking around for his keys so he could leave for work.

"Bye, Dad." I plant a quick kiss on his cheek. He smiles at me with love in his eyes. I've missed that. I give him a spontaneous fierce hug too.

"You okay, Rosey?"

"Yeah, just glad to see you. How about I make dinner tonight and we can catch up? I've got a surprise for you."

"You couldn't tell me last night?"

I frown, "Not really for public consumption."

He looks worried all of a sudden, "Rose, you're not… you're not in any kind of trouble are you?"

"No! It's a good surprise, I promise. Stop worrying." I mentally gloss over the fact that I am in some kind of trouble with his best friend. That's not what he has nightmares about.

"But I'm so good at it." He smirks and I laugh as he intended.

"Well, I'm not pregnant, not on drugs, not moving to another continent, not sick, what else can you come up with?"

"I'll let you know. Love you, Rosey."

"Love you too. Don't be late, they'll dock your pay." They won't. They underpay him and they know it.

He waves a banana in my direction and heads out the door.

I wander around my childhood home a little aimlessly. I've never felt like a stranger in my own house, obviously. But for the first time, I feel like it's no longer my home. Not someplace I feel comfortable making changes or rearranging the furniture. So I head back to my room and try to plot out this looming novel.

It has to be about a gorgeous billionaire. Most of my books have one, and while I need to mix things up, the publisher is expecting something that at least fits in with my other books. And the hero can't bear any resemblance to Aiden. So not tall and sculpted with a Mr. Darcy personality. I sigh heavily. I am so team Darcy. I'm not sure I have what it takes to write a Bingley romance. *Well, I'd better find it.* I tell myself sternly. No more excuses. I decide I'll rewatch a few favorite movies. Maybe one of the characters will give me some inspiration in terms of what direction to go.

Downstairs in the living room, I pull out the drawer full of DVDs. Believe it or not, there are even a few VHS tapes in there, not that there's anything to play them on. That's how attached Dad gets to some things. I've tried to get him into streaming, but he resists with every fiber of his being.

I grin as I flip through the titles. A lot of these were my mom's. I laugh and cry my way through *Ya Ya Sisterhood*, feeling a little bit better about the state of my life when the end credits roll. I make myself some lunch and carry my plate of triple cheese sandwiches and potato chips (I'm on vacation!) back to the couch and load up *Failure to Launch*. It's funny, but I'm not inspired yet.

"Oh, shit." I finally looked at a clock. Dad will be home in an hour or so and I haven't started dinner. I put away the movies and rush into the kitchen so I can figure out what to make that will be quick and still feel like a celebration.

I finally decide on baked tortellini with garlic bread. All the carbs and cheese will soothe Dad's heart, not in a medical way, that's for sure. And there's just enough time to make chocolate cupcakes for dessert.

I get busy, the steam from cooking making stray wisps of my hair curl into small corkscrews. I'm just frosting the cupcakes, which are still a little warm so the frosting is melting a little, but Dad won't mind. Then I hear his car in the driveway.

He comes in much as he left, a little absent-minded with a warm smile for me. Then he sees the spread of food, "You sure you're not in trouble, Rosey?"

"I'm sure. But what did your imagination come up with?"

"You're going to head to the inner city to teach underprivileged kids while living in a rat-infested apartment?"

I snort, "Noble but I don't have that kind of patience and you know it."

"For the kids or the rats?"

"Either, but definitely not both in the same day."

He goes over to the sink and washes his hands. Then takes his seat at the table, "So when are you going to tell me?"

"When you've gone halfway into a cheese coma," I announce cheerfully.

"Rose. Just out with it."

I put the baking dish of tortellini on its trivet in the middle of the table. It smells divine and really, who can be depressed when they catch a whiff of tomatoey cheesy goodness? "Fine, remember when I told you I'd gotten a scholarship?"

"Yes..." He's looking at me with concern.

"Well, that was a bit of white lie. I actually started an online business. I sort of fell into it by accident, but it's done really well."

Dad is frowning, "not one of those sleazy places selling cheap knockoffs?"

"No. Where do you come up with this stuff? It's to do with online publishing. You know all those ebooks you refuse to read?" I admit this is still a bit of a white lie, but if I tell Dad I'm an author, he *will* read my stuff and then all hell will break loose. I'd meant to write a couple of things under another pen name as a decoy, but I never got around to it.

He's still not looking happy, "But what about school. I wanted you to be able to study without worrying about money."

"Dad. It was something I fell into. It started as a fun thing, and then I started making money. Which I really enjoy. Enough money that I paid off the mortgage last week." I gulp, waiting for his reaction.

"What mortgage?"

"This one. The house is yours, Dad. All you have to do is pay the taxes, which is probably just as bad."

He sits back in his chair, looking stunned. "That's not first job kind of money, Rose."

I shrug. "Things have changed. Free economy, high school entrepreneurs. I promise I'm not in debt and I still have enough money to look at buying my own place. But I don't need you to worry — about me or the house."

"I'm stunned. That is not what I was expecting."

"I know." I grin. "No rats. So will you go on that fishing trip with Aiden, please? I don't want to hear any excuses."

He's looking at me like I grew up without him noticing *and* turned into something completely alien.

"Okay." He nods decisively. "I still wish you'd put the money into savings."

"Knew you'd say that."

"Then why didn't you do it?"

"Because you're a good guy, Dad, and you deserve something nice for once. If I'd offered to buy you a new car, you'd tell me yours is perfectly fine."

"It is."

"This gift is harder to return." I smile smugly at him, which makes him roll his eyes.

"Lastly, I'm going to head out tomorrow and spend a few weeks at the beach. I promise I'll be back to visit some more. This way you can decompress."

He eats an entire piece of garlic bread before he answers. "You grew up on me, Rose. I'm not sure how I missed it. Your mom would be so proud of you."

My eyes get a little misty at that. I'm not convinced she'd be that proud of how I've acquired the money. Although she always loved to read.

"Love you, Dad."

"Back at you, Rosey."

We eat, chatting about all kinds of stuff. Dad asks about Ingrid. He knows she has a conflicted relationship with her guardian but not all the details, so I have to censor what I say carefully, but I love that he remembers to ask.

We've never talked about my dad dating again. I know it's a possibility, and I think I'm mostly okay with it. I definitely want him to be happy, but it would be weird. He's never brought it up, and I'm not quite at the point of being ready to directly broach the subject with him. I suspect he likes not having to worry about anyone else when he comes home.

Dad loves the cupcakes. So much that he eats two and then says, "You sure you need to rush off, Rosey? I could use a few more of these." He smiles at the platter with only six cupcakes remaining.

"I'm sure. But how about I make a couple of batches in the morning and stick them in the freezer for you? That way you can pull one out when you need it."

He looks delighted, so I mentally delay my departure by a few hours tomorrow. Things like this make me think I should settle closer to him, where I could swing by and leave cupcakes in his freezer once a week.

When I head up to my room for the night, I bring the window blinds back up. There's no danger of seeing Aiden since he's not here, and I always like as much light as I can get, even at night. Okay, not blaring street lights in my window but softer lighting, moonlight — enough to stumble to the bathroom without having to turn something on.

I'm nervous about which Aiden I'm going to find at the cabin. The stern commander who looks like his face might crack if he smiles or the laid-back Aiden that's not really all that laid back when compared to other people? But at least that one is willing to lean back in a chair and drink a beer with an old buddy.

But his old buddy won't be there. I've never spent more than a few minutes alone with Aiden, and I'm nervous. I have no idea what to expect. Which is why I need to let go of this crush I have on him because clearly, I don't really know him all that well.

And yet still I find myself lying in my small bed, my fingers between my thighs, rubbing, pressing while I imagine those firm lips on my breasts. I cum with a sharply held breath and a long sigh. It's not enough. It's never really been enough, just something that gets me by. The scent of my arousal hangs in the air as I curl up in a ball and try to get some sleep.

In the morning, I make sure I'm downstairs before Dad goes to work, even though I'm still half asleep. I give him several long hugs and make sure he has a cupcake with him to perk up his lunch. Then I head back upstairs and take a quick shower. I toss all my clothes and sheets in the laundry so they'll be done before I leave and then head into the kitchen.

I eat breakfast while I bake. A few sips of coffee and a nibble of an English muffin while the mixer beats the butter and sugar together and then a banana while the oven preheats. Yes, I should have done that first, but sometimes coffee is needed to kickstart those brain cells.

When the cupcakes are in the oven, I transfer the laundry to the dryer and do a double check upstairs that I have everything in my bag. The house is smelling really good. I stuck with chocolate because they're Dad's favorite, and I don't want to experiment when I'm not around to see if he likes the results. I have to take a few shortcuts because of the time, so I stick the whole pan of cupcakes in the freezer to chill for a few minutes. I made the frosting while I was waiting for the timer to go. When I think they're cold enough, I give them a generous gob of frosting and stick them back in the freezer while I take my bags out to the car. Then I pack the cold, frosted cupcakes into containers that I label with some food labels I got Dad for Christmas, which apparently he's never used, and leave three on a plate in the fridge for him. I think that's it. And the clock says it's getting past time to go if I want to be up the mountain before dark.

I lock up the house, double-checking the sliding door, and head out.

The first part of the trip is boring because I've spent years driving up and down these roads. The only thing that ever changes is that they get more congested and there's even fewer interesting things to look at as more strip malls spring up. Sometimes an old furniture store will get replaced with a big box store, but that's not the kind of thing that captures my interest.

When I exit the freeway onto the rural highway, the views open up. Sometimes it's hard to believe that this too is California because it seems to be either from another century or another state. Long rolling fields and pasturelands. Small historic churches and 'something important happened here' markers. I can't imagine who wouldn't prefer this to breathing exhaust all day.

11

Rose

I'm not sure how Aiden got my cell phone number. I probably don't want to know. And it's not like it bothers me that he has it. I couldn't offer it up, obviously. That would look like I was flirting or hoping for something. Which I'm not. In any event, I find a text message waiting for me when I stop at what passes for shopping in the tiny mountain community of San Sebastian. It's really just a wide spot in the road with a general store slash grocery, a seedy bar, and a gas station that also does pizza carryout and ice cream in the summer. The text message just says,

> Let me know when you're arriving.

There's no 'Hey, this is Aiden' or a signature or anything. And yet I know. Instead of replying, I hit call and wait through what seems like a hundred rings. Finally, he picks up with, "Rose? You aren't running out on me, are you?"

"Um, no. Do you want me to? I'm just at the shopping center. Do you need anything from the grocery store?"

His voice softens slightly, "No, we're good for food. I stocked up as I was leaving the city. So unless there's something you can only find at Fred's, I have plenty for both of us."

"Oh. Okay. Well then, I guess I'll see you in twenty." I can't hold in the nervous laugh. I really don't have a clear picture of how this is going to go.

"Be careful on the way up. There were a couple of washouts last winter from the looks of things. If I don't see you in thirty minutes, I'll come looking."

"Okay. See you soon." I hang up. A little warmed by his concern. My car isn't really ideal for unpaved mountain roads and the cell service is nonexistent between this parking lot and the cabin. Since I don't need to get groceries, I fill up the tank, use the restroom and treat myself to a strawberry milkshake. That's a classified secret of San Seb's because tourists think it's made from ordinary strawberry ice cream, but it's not. They use homemade vanilla ice cream and add in locally grown fresh strawberries. There's nothing in this world that tastes quite like it.

I secure my treat in the cup holder and fasten my seatbelt. Time to finish facing my demons or punishment or whatever the hell this is.

The road *is* bumpy. And there are a couple of spots where I have to fight the steering wheel to keep from spinning into the ruts. Kevin's engine isn't happy about the steep grade and my stomach is knotting tighter the closer I get to the cabin. Thankfully, I don't have to deal with any oncoming traffic. But at least the inside of the car smells of crushed strawberries and that lifts my spirits.

There are five other cabins on this side of the mountain, but they're rarely occupied, just like ours. The last time I was up here was the summer after my freshman year, right before

Darla was born. Dad and I came up for a week. It was a good trip, but we both felt awkward being here without Mom. Like we didn't quite know what to do with ourselves. Which was silly because she didn't particularly like the cabin and would mostly sack out with a paperback until it was time to leave. She wasn't mean about it, but she was all city. Somehow, not having her being a lump on the couch felt wrong. We left a couple of days early.

I think Dad's been back since but only as a pure escape and I'm guessing he brought work with him in the form of all his medical journals he's forever complaining he doesn't have time to read. And once, when he lost a patient he was really close to. I'd offered to come home for that one, but he told me not to.

I didn't like lying to him about where I was going. I know it's not exactly truthful to not tell him about Darla, but my conscience has a fairly clear line between lies of omission and those of commission. Telling him I'm going to the beach is well into the uncomfortable category. I sigh. Too late now. I'm here and there's Aiden's giant truck dominating the small clearing. I pull up to the side and get out with my milkshake, which I set on the roof of my car. I'll get my luggage later.

I shake out my legs. I'm more than a little tight from that tense drive up the mountain. So I stretch and bend until the door opens.

"Stop stalling, Rose. I've got dinner ready."

I bounce up from my deep bend, seeing stars from the sudden elevation change. "You didn't have to do that."

"This place doesn't exactly have staff, so yeah, I did. It wasn't any trouble to make it for two. Come on." He turns away but leaves the door open. I grab my milkshake and take a deep drag through the straw as I slowly follow him inside. I feel a lot like I've been called into the principal's office.

We sit down at the old round table that my parents found at a nearby estate sale. Aiden's made a really amazing meal of penne pasta with sun-dried tomatoes, fresh vegetables, and some kind of fancy cheese.

"This is really good," I say with surprise after the first few bites. "I didn't know you could cook."

He looks at me with a slight smirk, "There's a lot you don't know about me, Rose. Part of why you're here." He frowns down at his plate. "I did a load of wash when I got here, so there are clean sheets for you to set up in the loft. Take this evening to get settled. We'll talk in the morning about what I'm expecting from you."

I gulp, "I didn't know you had any expectations." Fuck. Maybe I should have clarified a few things before agreeing to spend time in the cabin with him, alone.

His face settles into stern lines, every inch the military officer, "Get used to it, kid. This is not your vacation."

12

____

Rose

After dinner, I take my plate and water glass into the kitchen, planning to wash them, but Aiden takes them from me and shoos me towards the loft. I ignore that and go out to my car to get my bags. The cabin is small, designed that way to make it heat efficient in the winter. And in the summer nobody wants to be inside anyway, so it doesn't really matter. Before, I always felt like there was plenty of space, but somehow *his* presence makes the place feel smaller than it is. We've yet to talk about the elephant in the room.

The whole cabin always has this dry pine smell, it wafts off the nearby forest and luckily I love it and am not allergic. But today all I can smell is Aiden. It's a woodsy-citrusy smell that I absolutely adore. Every time I get a whiff, I want to stop and do some deep breathing. I've tried for years to figure out what aftershave he uses without actually asking because that would be weird. As if wanting some so I can spray it on my sheets isn't.

I wonder what it would be like if we were here together for some other reason and he wasn't aware I had a crush on him? Would it still be awkward and uncomfortable? A little, I decide. But nothing like this. Right now I'm embarrassed on so many levels I no longer know what precisely is making me blush.

I drag my bags inside and drop them in the middle of the floor. There's a rough-hewn ladder leading up to the sleeping loft that overhangs the living room. I'm used to it because this was always my room. When I thought I was coming up here by myself, I indulged in a few fantasies of sleeping in a real bed, but it's not the first time my dreams have gone poof like a soap bubble.

When I have everything upstairs (there's only so much weight I can sling over my shoulder before I topple backward, so it takes a few trips), I quickly make up the twin mattress that's fitted under the eves. I stow my bags in the corner by the railing and collect my toiletries to take back down and stash in the bathroom. Sharing a bathroom with Aiden. What has my world come to?

What I am pretty clear on is that he doesn't want to indulge in idle chitchat. The message that I should keep to myself and stay out of his way was kinda hard to miss. I'm not sure I'm ready to comply though. I should have brought wine. Since I didn't, a cup of tea will have to do. The heat of the day is gone, and the sun is low on the horizon — or at least as much of it as I can see with the mountain and all. Basically, it's almost sunset and I intend to lounge on the back deck to watch it.

I head back down the ladder, store my toiletries in the cupboard in the bathroom, and head into the kitchen. There's an old-fashioned whistling kettle that I fill and set on the stove, then I poke around in the cupboards for a tea bag.

"Looking for something?"

I jump. Aiden is right behind me, closer than he's come all evening.

"A tea bag. There used to be a giant tin in here somewhere."

"Try this." He hands me a box of individually packaged silk sachets that promise the wonders of high alpine herbs.

"Um, okay, but I'd be happy with Lipton's."

"I cleaned out all the old and expired stuff. If all you want is colored water…"

I sigh and take one of his fancy things. At least my favorite mug from childhood in the shape of a pink flamingo is still in the cupboard. I grab it and smile with the familiar feel of it in my hands. When the water boils I pour it over the fancy tea bag, full of life-giving shit, and turn around. I'm not entirely sure if Aiden is still standing there since I was doing my best to ignore him.

He's not. He's sitting at the dining room table with stacks of reading material. I peek as I walk by — *Journal of Rural Health*, about a year's worth of back copies of the *Lancet*. In other words, fun stuff. I roll my eyes and head out onto the deck. I settle into one of the wooden lounge chairs that nobody ever bothers to bring inside so they're worn gray. The roof over-hangs though, so they don't get too wet or snowy. The sun is just hitting that blazing phase where it's extra bright, but there aren't any pretty colors yet. It's partially blocked by the stand of lodge pines, but that's part of the charm. There's some sleepy chittering of birds as they head back to their nests or make one last foray to feed hungry babies, then it all goes beautifully silent.

Finally, I take a sip of the tea. It's not that bad. I'll never admit it and I'm definitely not blowing cash on it myself, but if Aiden wants to waste his money, I'm willing to go along. On this, anyway.

The sun dips down with streaks of coral and deeper gold appearing. I sigh in frustration when Aiden flips on the over-head light in the dining room. Do I dare?

Yes, I rather think I do.

Aiden

Fuck. I can't concentrate, and I have only myself to blame. What was I thinking telling Rose to come to the cabin? I knew I was in trouble when I watched her cheeks hollow as she sucked on that damn straw from her milkshake in the driveway. Her hair is somewhat tamed into a long, loose braid that makes my fingers itch. Mostly to spank her for putting these thoughts in my head, even though I can't say she's done anything recently to draw attention to herself.

I'm the one that told her to take the loft. I know she's always slept up there, so she didn't seem too surprised. But I didn't think about having to watch her round little ass as she went up and down the ladder. Again and again and again. *She's still a kid by comparison*, I keep telling myself. *I'm the grown-up.*

Which is why I'm trying to catch up on reading material. I really need to take advantage of the time before I start my new position, but I'm sitting here now instead of relaxing with a beer because I've got to take my mind off of Rose.

Until the overhead light goes out. "Fuck." I swear under my breath, prepared to go on a hunt for a new light bulb. Until I hear a smothered giggle behind me.

"Come on, Commander. You're spoiling the sunset. Hurry up, we don't have all day."

That's when I notice she's trying to tug me out of the chair. For some odd reason, I let her. She leads me out on the deck and pushes me towards one of the lounge chairs.

"Sit. You can go back to your boring reading in another fifteen minutes."

"Rose..."

She raises her eyebrows at me like I'm failing some kind of test. The sunset really is gorgeous. The cabin is perched about halfway up the mountain, so as the sun sinks over the horizon you're looking down on it with even more sky visible than at sea level. I shut up and lean back in the chair, swatting at the occasional bug trying to make a meal of me.

When the last of the color has faded, Rose gets up and heads towards the screen door. "There, that wasn't so bad, was it?"

"No, it was lovely. I need to do that more often."

Her smile practically glows in the dimming light as she heads inside. I sit for a few minutes more, knowing I need to establish some firm ground rules for myself as much as her. Or I'm going to have her under me before the week is out. My cock is once again reminding me that it's been too long. And that it would rather explore Rose's pussy than any other it's encountered in quite a while. Fuck it all.

I head back inside and force myself to read until I find I've read the same page over five times and couldn't tell you anything it said. Rose already went up to bed so I get up from the table, turn off the light, and head into the cabin's one bedroom.

13

Rose

The intoxicating scent of perfectly brewed coffee wakes me up. For a moment, I'm simply warm and comfortable in a quiet room with the promising smell of life-giving sustenance when I open my eyes. I smile and snuggle into my pillow for just a few more seconds. Then I remember. It's not Ing making coffee because Ing doesn't even drink coffee. She's a cola in the morning kind of girl, which I've never been able to understand. If I want coffee, I'm going to have to see Aiden and at some point let him lecture me on all his rules for the next few weeks. Ugh.

I roll out of bed and reluctantly find some jeans and a long-sleeve t-shirt to put on. I back down the ladder and only when I'm firmly on the ground do I look around. He's nowhere in sight, but I hear some rustling coming from the kitchen area so he must still be in there finding something in one of the lower cabinets. I sigh and head into the bathroom to brush my teeth and wash my face. I want a shower at some point today, but for some reason, I'm too nervous to do it while Aiden's in the cabin. Guess I'm going to have to get over that one soon or he'll think I'm more than a few screws loose.

A polite smile is pasted on my face as I go in search of the coffee. Aiden stands in front of the stove stirring something. He's not shaved yet, and the dark stubble is looking absolutely divine. I sigh in admiration of the delectable picture he makes, and he looks up at me, his blue eyes narrowing slightly.

"Morning, Rose. Oatmeal will be on the table in just a minute."

I make a face. I hate oatmeal. "I'll just have toast."

"You'll have oatmeal. You need fuel and I don't want to hear any excuses that you were tired later. There's sugar or maple syrup if that makes it more palatable."

Right, guess I'm having oatmeal. His face is telling me this is not the thing to go to war over because I won't win and it might make everything else worse. If this is any sign of what's coming, I'm in for a hell of a month. I grab a mug and fill it from the carafe on the counter, inhaling deeply before taking a grateful sip. So damn good. I might have moaned. Something caught Aiden's attention because he's glaring at me. Great. I take myself out of his space and go sit at the table.

A bowl of oatmeal appears in front of me, along with a spoon. I stare at it with disdain. I thought part of being an adult was getting to eat what you want and suffering the consequences. Of course, Aiden has yet to acknowledge I'm an adult. Perhaps if he forces oatmeal on me for thirty days it will cure me of my crush? I cheer up at the thought and reach for the sugar bowl and the milk. I can practically hear Aiden frowning as I ladle on two generous spoonfuls of sugar. "Stop glaring, I'm eating the oatmeal, a little sugar won't hurt me."

"If you knew what…"

I interrupt him, "Life was really all about? It's not preventing death at all costs, Aiden. Relax, live a little. If a little sugar makes you smile, that alone might just make you live longer."

He opens his mouth to say something but then shuts it again. Sticking his spoon into his sugar-free oatmeal and proceeding to eat it like it's a military exercise. Efficient, economic, and boring as hell.

Aiden needs me. He doesn't know it yet, but he does. And I don't mean sexually (unfortunately). I see now that fate has brought us together so he can freaking *lighten up*. I smile with anticipation. This will be fun.

My smile fades though when I glance across the table to find him glaring at me. Again. "What now?" I ask sweetly.

"Now we talk about how this is going to go. Or rather I talk and you listen."

I raise both my eyebrows, "Oh, really?"

He gets up to take his bowl to the sink and refill his coffee cup. There's no humor in his eyes when he starts in, but it's clear he's so used to giving orders he doesn't feel the need to raise his voice either, "I will take care of the cooking and you will do dishes and clean the counters. In between that, I expect your ass glued to that chair over there until you've written at least five thousand words every day. None of which will feature anyone that resembles me."

"I don't know how to write lesbian romance," I say snarkily. It doesn't go over well if his eye roll is anything to judge by.

"I can add chopping wood to your chore list if you like?"

I groan, nobody wants me near an axe, at least not without a hospital nearby. "Fine."

"And when the manuscript is complete, I will read and approve it before you hit publish."

I nod, I don't have a problem with that. I can promise you I'd be too embarrassed to base the main character on Aiden at this point, anyway. Although, what I'm going to do instead still eludes me. And I'm not thrilled that I'm acting like a bratty princess. It's not my usual style; I just can't seem to resist baiting Aiden.

I have to admit that the oatmeal was filling without being heavy. And that it was sort of nice to have someone besides Dad wanting me to take care of myself. I'm just not sure if Aiden feels that way about the entire human race. I mean, I'm sure he does, that's why he became a doctor, but would he push oatmeal on *them* so relentlessly if any of them were sitting across the table? I honestly don't know. And I'm a little afraid to find out.

Aiden

I'm glad Rose isn't fighting me on my rules because I'm seriously on edge after her breathy little moans over coffee, of all things. I'm sorely tempted to throw her over my shoulder and give in to what my cock clearly wants. It's been hard enough to pound nails ever since she came down the ladder, and I need to put some distance between her and me stat. If I can get her to stay in one place with her laptop, then I can go chop wood until my cock gives up the fight and acknowledges that sinking into Rose is never going to happen. Then maybe I'll be able to get some reading in, so I at least have some semblance of a strategic plan for my new job.

I leave Rose to do the dishes and go take a shower. I need to shave and remind myself that I am not a mountain man, at least not for more than a week or two at a time. When I emerge, she's fidgeting at the small desk. I can see her screen over her shoulder and it's completely blank. "What's the matter, you must have some ideas?"

"I have ideas, they're just not jelling into a story. I need to know the characters better."

I've never written anything more creative than a five-year plan. I wish I could help her find her new direction without stressing about it but I'm clueless so I shrug and head outside to work on restocking the woodpile. It's not needed now but come autumn it will be an important backup if the power goes out which it frequently does up here.

I keep myself busy outdoors until I can't put lunch off any longer. I've chopped and stacked wood until my shoulders are sore, cleared brush from the trail that leads to the small lake, and made a list of supplies to get for patching some of the loose siding. The manual labor feels good.

When I head inside, I'm sweaty and hot. Wood chips and pine needles have worked their way down the back of my shirt and are starting to itch. It doesn't occur to me that pulling my shirt off is a problem until I hear Rose inhale sharply. When I look over, her gaze is slightly glassy and glued to my chest. I can't help feeling a little bit smug about that. I shrug it off as fast as I can, still wondering how Rose's mind works. In the bedroom, I pull a clean t-shirt out of my bag and tug it over my head and then head into the kitchen to make sandwiches.

I'm half expecting her to complain about the food again, I made some simple tuna fish and spinach sandwiches on whole grain but she eats it like she can't taste it so it doesn't matter. That doesn't seem like her, but maybe writers get this way when they're working. As soon as she's done, she heads back to the computer and I decide to take my journals outside to the deck. Maybe the fresh air will make them easier to read.

Certainly, I get a little further than I did before, but I find myself frequently stopping and wondering how Rose is getting on. And every now and then I take in the same view that held the sunset we watched last night and remember how nice it was to simply pause and appreciate.

In a weird way, I like that Rose is having trouble thinking up a hero that's not me. Twisted, but there it is. Guess I'm more of a narcissist than I ever gave myself credit for. Maybe I should find some kind of excuse to send her home early. Let her off the hook for the day-to-day stuff and just preview everything at the end. I should, but I'm not going to. At the very least, she'll know just how boringly human I am. I force myself to go back to a study of life expectancy among rural citizens. It's depressing enough to suit my mood.

14

***

Rose

This is not working. I have two pages of total crap on the screen. None of it is usable, not really. I thought that if I got something, anything, down then the words might flow. But then Aiden came in and did that sexy move of pulling his shirt off with one hand from the back, and I melted into a little puddle of goo. Now all I can think or see or smell is him. Anything I write at the moment is going to star Aiden.

There's only one solution — I need to get out of here. Temporarily, at the very least. And at least one thing has changed since the last time I was up here. I'm now over twenty-one. Which means I can go into the bar at the bottom of the mountain. It's seedy, but there are bound to be guys there that bear zero resemblance to my handsome surgeon. And I mean zero. The few times I've driven past after dark there were usually two rows of motorcycles, and the rest of the parking lot were oversized trucks. Not the neat, pretty kind like Aiden's. More the mudding in the woods after a full day logging type of truck.

And just because I go in doesn't mean I have to drink — plus it's mid-afternoon. If I get there when they open at five, I can get some ideas down on my phone and be back up here before it's completely dark. I'm liking this idea. Even if a tiny part of me feels like I'm betraying Aiden somehow. I'm not. He asked me (okay, insisted) I write about someone else, and I'm going to make my best effort to make that happen for him. I owe it to myself too.

When I pop my head around the door out to the deck to tell him I'm headed out, I can tell he's asleep. He looks relaxed but exhausted. If I wake him up, he'll go back to work. So I tiptoe over and slide his reading glasses off his nose and set them on the table. He's the sexiest thing alive when he has those glasses on. Then I write him a quick note on the adjacent legal pad, so hopefully, he sees it when he wakes up. Or maybe he'll still be asleep when I get back. Wouldn't that be a hoot?

I head back inside and grab my purse. I'm not taking my laptop, this is just a reconnaissance and research mission. I can take notes on my phone. I'm humming along to my favorite pop star as I drive down the mountain. It is so much more fun going down than up. Takes no gas at all and the sunlight is filtering beautifully through the trees.

I'm quaking just a little when I park in front of the bar. There are bigger, nastier looking bikes here than I remember. But I'm a grown-up businesswoman, I will not be scared off by a few tough guys. I don't need Aiden laughing at me over that. Not that he would, I can't think of a time when he's ever laughed at me. Maybe an occasional twinkle in his eyes, but I can forgive him that much.

I pull open the heavy steel door, and the odor of stale beer and peanut shells almost overwhelms me. I let my eyes adjust to the interior gloom and notice that the place has gone silent. I keep a five-dollar bill in a separate pocket of my purse for any occasion where I don't feel safe pulling my wallet out, and I reach for it now. I find an open spot at the bar and ask the bartender for a cola. He looks at me funny but exchanges the drink for the money without asking for my ID. Which in theory he should do since you aren't supposed to be in here at all if you're underage but judging by the clientele I don't think he's too worried. And if I were with the cops trying to trick him, I'd be asking for liquor, right?

I see a quiet table at the back where I can have my back against the wall. That seems to be a favored aspect, because most of the middle tables in the room are empty. I take out my phone and pretend I'm scrolling through social media until the conversations pick back up again, and then I raise my head to look around.

I hate to be rude, but this is not romance hero material. Particularly not when a few of them come up to me, wanting to know what my hourly rate is. Oh. Dear. God.

After the fifth such innuendo, I've decided I've had enough and get up to leave. Nobody tries to stop me, so I'm breathing a sigh of relief when I step out of the bar onto the sidewalk. More time had passed than I thought because the sun is going down. And I shouldn't have relaxed my guard. I really shouldn't have.

I didn't even see him. All I know is something big slammed me against the rough boards of the building and then dragged me up. I screamed as best I could around the hand holding my throat as my back scraped against the wood. Not much noise came out, so I didn't miss the words, "Fucking little bitch. Nobody turns me down, you sorry piece of ass. And you ain't going to after I'm done with you either."

I'm trying to kick him. I'm trying to breathe and scream, but he's dragging me through the bushes towards his truck. I panic and try to reach his eyes with my keys that are still clutched in my hand. I can't reach, but it annoys him enough that he screams at me again. I don't know if someone called or if the deputy was driving by, but out of nowhere, there's a gun pointed at giant murdering guy's head, "Put the girl down, Malone. You know the drill."

Unfortunately, he doesn't really, or he just doesn't like following orders because he drops me right onto the crushed gravel of the parking lot and I land hard. Still beats being raped and murdered.

Once big murdering guy, who the deputy seems to know as Malone, is in handcuffs, the deputy helps me to my feet. "You alright there, Miss? Need an ambulance?"

"Um, I don't think so, but he really scraped me up."

"Yeah, sorry about that. He's only been out on parole for twelve hours."

What the fuck? They *let* this guy out?

"I'll need to get a statement from you, but if you can write down your local address, I can come see you for it later."

Oh, hell no. "I'd rather just write it out for you now. You probably saw more than I did."

He gives me a sad half-smile and fetches a clipboard out of his vehicle. It's painful, but I bend over the hood and fill out the form. I really didn't see much, so it doesn't take too long. I don't give him my local address. Anyone that needs more can contact me through official channels like my email. But I also know I'm in no state to drive back up the mountain, so I rub my aching throat and pull out my cell phone to text Aiden.

> At the bar down the hill. Can you come get me?

> Why? Have you been drinking?

> No. Had an accident. Don't think I should drive.

He'll know as soon as he sees me, but I don't want him doing something stupid coming down the mountain and wrapping around a tree.

Be right there

I sigh and lean against one of the posts holding up the front of the building. I don't want to sit down right now, and all of me is hurting worse with every passing second. The bad guy is now handcuffed in the backseat of the deputy's vehicle, and the deputy, whose name is Mark Healy, offers to wait with me until Aiden shows up. Which is about ten seconds later. He leaps out of his truck, "Rose? What the hell happened?"

Even yelling I'm so happy to see him, tears start running down my cheeks. "I'm mostly okay, Aiden."

He doesn't look like he believes me.

"Rose, you okay for me to leave?" Deputy Healey asks, and I give him a smile or as best as I can manage. "Yes. Aiden will take care of me. Thanks for waiting."

"Wait, who did this to her?" Aiden asks.

"The guy in the backseat of the squad car, who's headed back to prison tonight. She already filed her statement and declined medical treatment so the rest is lawyers and paperwork."

"Fuck."

The deputy just nods in understanding and gets into his vehicle.

Aiden turns back to me, and the expression in his eyes is heartbreaking. "Okay, Rose, let's get you taken care of. Can you walk or should I pick you up?"

"Walking probably won't hurt as much." I try to joke, but it's clear he's not in a laughing mood.

15

———

Rose

Aiden lifts me into his truck, his touch surprisingly gentle. He reaches around me to fasten the seatbelt. I try not to cry out when it rubs against some of the sore spots, but he notices, anyway. "Sorry, Rosebud. We'll get you taken care of as soon as possible." He shuts the door and goes around to the driver's side.

He climbs in and sits there quietly for a minute. Without turning his head towards me, he asks, "Rose? Either I take us back to the cabin and check you over myself or... I can take you into Carterville where there's a small hospital and a nurse can do it."

"Why...Why would we go to a hospital? Do you think it's that bad?" I'm scared now and shivering, even though the night is warm.

"No, I don't." He answers softly. "But, it means taking your clothes off in front of me. I'll need to check you over completely. This is a long way from a professional situation. If you're not comfortable with that, I completely understand."

"No. I mean, I'd rather it was you."

"You sure?"

I nod, but then remember he's not looking my way. I'm still not sure why. "Yes, I trust you, Aiden."

He mutters something that sounds like 'glad one of us does' but I may have misheard. His jaw clenches as he starts the engine and pulls away from the bar and shopping center. I'm not sure I'll ever be able to stop here again. Definitely not at night.

Aiden notices my shivering and turns on the heat a little. I'm still clasping my elbows tight, trying to hold everything together. The drive back up the mountain is silent. When he parks the truck, he finally turns towards me briefly, "Wait here." Then he's out and unlocking the cabin. He leaves the door ajar and comes back to the truck. He carries me inside like I weigh nothing and heads straight into the bathroom where he sets me down on the counter.

I watch as he turns on the small wall heater and then briefly leaves returning with a folded t-shirt and some extra washcloths.

"We're going to start at the top and work our way down, okay?"

"Okay." I cast my eyes towards the floor, embarrassed and miserable that he's having to take care of me like the little girl he's been claiming I am.

His long elegant fingers loosen my hair and then do a survey of my scalp. When he finds the big lump he whistles softly, "That one is going to hurt for a while. I'll get you some ice for it in a minute." He leans over me to look at the back of my neck. I breathe him in and something in me relaxes just a smidge.

Aiden reaches in the drawer of the vanity and pulls out a pair of scissors. "Sorry, Rose, but this shirt is already toast." I nod and he cuts it off of me. I could have pulled it over my head, but my shoulder is already hurting and I'm not sure what that would do to it. He reaches behind me and unclasps my bra, pulling it off and folding it neatly on the vanity next to my hip. I'm now officially naked in front of Aiden McBride and the world hasn't ended. Yet.

He dabs carefully at the abrasions on my front, gently lifting each breast to check the skin underneath. Thank God that's mostly fine, as I don't think I could take him touching me even more right there. He turns all of me slightly on the vanity so he can see my back more clearly. He sucks in a breath. "Sorry, sweetness. You've got several splinters back here that need to come out."

He reaches into the drawer again, pulling out a pair of tweezers and sets to work. Even though it stings and occasionally downright hurts, the pressing of his fingers on my bare skin has my pussy fluttering with excitement. I try clenching my thighs to stop it, but that only seems to make things worse.

"Rose, have you had a tetanus shot lately?"

"Um, two years ago, I think?"

"You think or you know?"

"I know I've had one after I left for college, and I think it was two years ago."

"Well, that's some good news then. Okay, I've gotten everything I can for right now. There might be a few small ones in deep that will work their way out in the next few days. I'll have to check again tomorrow. The good news is you can now put this shirt on and cover up. The bad news is it's time for your lower half."

I appreciate he's at least trying to make light of it, and he helps me slip his t-shirt on over my sore shoulder. It's huge on me, and I'm guessing that's why he didn't try to find one of mine.

"Arms around my neck, okay?" I'm going to lift you up and slide your skirt and panties off."

I do as he asks, clinging tighter as I feel the air on my bare ass. He slides a folded towel onto the vanity before lowering me down and turning to my legs. There's more actual scratches here, and he carefully cleans each one, even checking the soles of my feet.

"Are you sure nothing happened, Rose? He didn't rape you?"

"No, he didn't have time."

"Will it be okay if I take a look? I'll feel better."

I half-smile at that, but I part my legs and lean back against his arm when he tells me to. He'll see I'm wet, so very wet, but that's because of him. I can tell when he notices because his arm at my back tenses and he draws a swift breath in, but he says nothing. A few seconds later and he pushes my knees together. "Okay, just one more thing to check, then you can go to bed."

He helps me down and directs me to bend over, my face cradled by my folded arms on the towel. My shoulder is screaming at me, but I don't think this will take very long. He runs a hand down each buttock, checking for lumps and splinters. If his hand lingers a little, I'm certainly not going to say anything.

"Okay. You're all set. Do you want to sleep down here tonight? I can take the loft."

"Actually… Can I sleep with you?"

"Rose…"

"I know… but I don't want to be alone right now. There's not really anyone else to ask."

He sighs heavily, "Fine, but don't say I didn't warn you this was a bad idea." For the first time tonight, I feel a genuine grin coming on.

"Go get in the bed, I'll bring you an ice pack for your head."

"I'll just brush my teeth first."

He nods and exits the small bathroom. I brush my teeth and swipe a comb through my hair, wishing I could braid it.

It's easy to see which side of the bed Aiden's been using. The stack of still unread medical journals is on the small nightstand, his sexy reading glasses perched on top. I get in on the other side of the queen-size bed, hoping his body heat will be enough to warm me up so this damn shivering can stop. It's not a big bed, I'll bet he has a bigger one at his place, but since I know nothing is going to happen, I don't think it really matters. I don't take up much space.

He comes into the bedroom with a bag of frozen peas and a small smile. "This will probably work better, just try not to sleep on them or we'll have peas everywhere." He places it on the top of my head and I grimace at the cold seeping into my scalp. I'm not sure I can last five minutes with that. Seems like a waste of vegetables.

16

Rose

Aiden is lying stiff as a board in the bed beside me. Like he's afraid he'll brush up against me and catch a fatal disease. Or that he's afraid of hurting me. I sigh and toss the bag of peas, now no longer frozen, on the nightstand. Parts of me are cold like my hands and feet while others are boiling over. My pussy is super excited to have her top candidate for the job in such close proximity. Seems to me the best solution for everyone is what I do next. I'm acting on instinct and impulse, and I'm not sorry.

I reach over and slide my hands under Aiden's t-shirt and flatten my palms against his abs. He jumps with a muttered, "Fuck, Rose!" and I giggle as I feel his perfectly toned muscles contract under my freezing fingers.

"Let me guess, your feet are cold too?" He asked with a resigned tone. I nod, but then remember he can't see me in the dark. "Yeah, but I didn't want to overstep." I'm teasing because I know he's not going to let me suffer.

He snorts, "Yeah, right. Okay, give them to me, princess. At least this time I'm braced for it."

"Really? You don't mind?"

"Not under the circumstances, but don't expect to make a habit of it."

My heart skips a beat at even the idea that I would ever be in the situation where such a habit could be formed. Like maybe this won't be the one and only time Aiden and I are in the same bed. My pussy clenches in excitement even though I should really tell her not to get her hopes up.

I slowly bring my feet over to where I think his calves must be. He reaches a hand down and positions them where he wants them against his legs. His skin is so warm. My toes curl in delight.

"Aiden?"

"Hmmm?"

"Why are you single?"

"Rose." The warning note in his voice is designed to warn me off, but I forge ahead anyway.

"I'm not asking with designs on your virtue. I just don't get it. You're good looking, you can cook, you're a decent guy so you must be single because you want to be. So why?"

"Why does that sound like an insult?"

"It's not. Basic curiosity. From the woman who's currently feeling you up." I grin into the dark.

"I'm single because I don't have the time or interest required for a long-term relationship."

"Like how my heroes start out," I say with satisfaction and a dreamy sigh.

"Not even close. Before I found the things that pointed specifically to you, I knew the Darla wasn't someone that knew me well."

"How?" Now I'm wondering what I missed.

His voice goes gravelly when he finally answers, "Because,

Rose, when I fuck a woman, she always cums before I do. Every single time. Usually two or three times. Now go to sleep."

I gulp, jealous beyond belief of any woman lucky enough to have his full attention in that way. I might be in his bed right now, but he's not worrying about my orgasms. Not by a long shot. He's tolerating my presence here right now and we all know it.

I'm still imagining what it would be like to be on the receiving end of his lovemaking. Not to mention trying to picture what three back-to-back orgasms would feel like (as he probably intended by mentioning it in the first place) when I finally fall asleep.

~

"Rose, wake up, baby."

Something is shaking my shoulder and as I groggily wake up to Aiden's voice, the nightmare recedes back where it came from.

"Shhh, sweetness. You're safe. Nobody's going to hurt you again."

He's holding me against his chest, his large palm smoothing the skin of my back underneath his t-shirt I'm still wearing. I groan as I shift onto my sore shoulder.

"Fuck. Hold on, Rosebud."

Aiden shifts us until he's on his back and I'm draped over his chest. It's an extremely interesting position, and I wish I were more awake to enjoy it.

"Better?"

"Mphh," I say into his pec.

His hands are still soothing me and I probably would have drifted off again if I hadn't noticed something hard pushing against my thigh. I still, afraid I'm misinterpreting something, but I definitely don't want to draw his attention to it. He'll be hightailing it out of the country before I can even make it to my car to chase after him if I do.

So I force my muscles to relax against him while I take this all in. Aiden's cock, at least, finds me attractive. Who knew? Is this why he's been so grumpy? Okay, I'm sure that's not the only reason. He smells divine. I don't know if it was all the wood chopping he was doing yesterday, but he smells like pine. Not the artificial kind, but the delicate scent of the forest.

"You smell good," I mumble into his chest and feel it move under me as he chuckles.

It dies when I press a soft kiss to his skin. "Thanks for taking care of me, Aiden. I know you don't want to, not really."

"That's not true, Rosebud. I do. But it wouldn't be good for you and that's more important."

That makes no sense, and my brain doesn't want to figure it out. So I instinctively wiggle down until Aiden's cock is slotted against the seam of my pussy. Despite the two layers of clothing between us, it feels right with my legs spread over his. I relax against him and despite one audible groan; he palms my ass to hold me there.

17

Aiden

I'm going to hell. Not just for the duration of the night while I hold Rose. I can feel every one of her sweet little wiggles as her body is determined to get up close and personal with my cock. Every time I try to shift her away, she snuggles down and ends up right back where she was. If I didn't have pants on, my eager and hard-as-nails cock would slip inside her right now with no effort on my part. Not going to happen.

No, instead I'm going to hell for thinking about just how good that would feel. For wondering about the possibility of keeping her forever. Holding her has been... eye-opening. I don't ever recall feeling like this with any other woman. Not my ex-wife, even back when I thought I liked her, or anyone since. I never felt this protective or fierce, like I would gladly slay dragons for her. That bastard that hurt her last night is lucky he was already in custody when I got there. If he hadn't been, he'd be in tiny pieces right now.

Rose is dreaming again, more pleasant ones this time, I

think. She's murmuring softly, her fingertips twitching lightly where they rest under her cheek against my chest. She's a delicious armful, and I know this bed is going to feel empty as fuck after tonight.

Eventually, I must fall asleep because I wake up at dawn. Rose is still sound asleep. She gives a breathy little moan of protest when I slip out from under her. She curls up again when I bring the covers up over her and tuck her in, and I take a moment to soak in her beauty. As quietly as I can, I leave the bedroom and go wash up. I need coffee and a few minutes alone to regain my equilibrium.

That lasts all of about five minutes, then Rose comes out to the deck to find me, still wearing my t-shirt, rubbing the sleep out of her eyes. Her hair is sexily mussed and my cock is back in action, hard as ever. Until I see her throat.

"Fuck, Rose."

"What?" Her eyes go wide with alarm so I put all my effort into gentling my voice.

"Come here." I tug her gently down onto my lap. I'm sitting in one of those Adirondack recliners so she fits nicely on my thighs. I push her hair back over her shoulders and touch the black and blue bruises on her throat. "Does that hurt?"

"Not your touch, no. It's a little sore to swallow."

"I'm so sorry, Rosebud."

"Not your fault. Well, it's sort of your fault." Her eyes are twinkling as she tries to lighten the mood.

"How so?"

"You're too distracting. I went down there to find some inspiration that wasn't you. If ever there was an anti-Aiden, he'd be in that bar."

"Did it work?" God, I hope not.

"No." She sighed. "Now I'm more behind than ever."

I pull her closer against my chest, offering her my coffee cup, which she takes eagerly. I'm a bastard. I'm basking in the knowledge that I'm the man she still thinks about. She's still attracted to me. I shouldn't be encouraging her, but I'm finding that more and more appealing as I acknowledge my feelings for her. I skate wide around that topic for now.

"Think of it this way. You need to write this book for my sister Linda."

"I didn't know you had a sister."

"I do. Two of them. Linda is the bossy one and, according to her, your biggest fan."

"Aw, that's so sweet."

"Apparently. Until she realized she was reading about her little brother's cock. She was not amused."

Rose chokes with laughter. "I can see how that would be awkward. Is she the one who…"

"Yes. She's the one that outed you. Well, she doesn't know it was you behind Darla, but yes. So you're really writing this next one for her."

"Hmmm. Is she married?"

"Yes, to a man named Todd."

"How'd they meet?"

"Rose, you can't…"

"Oh hush, I'm not going to write their story. But maybe if I craft a hero in the shape of what Linda appreciates, it will solve all these problems."

"He's in the Air Force." I try to keep the disdain out of my voice, but come on.

"And that's a bad thing?" She sounds skeptical.

"If he were smart, he'd have gone into the Navy. Otherwise, he's okay."

"So how'd they meet?" She asks again, handing me back the empty coffee mug and snuggling against me. I can't seem to stop my hands from playing with her hair.

"The story they both told me is that she met him in Vegas when he was there for a golf weekend and she went with friends for a bachelorette party. But a buddy of mine who knows Todd says they actually met when she locked herself in the restroom at a gas station on the Interstate and Todd rescued her."

"Oh, that's so sweet."

"It is?"

"Yes. It's perfect. Time to get to work." She leans up and kisses me full on the mouth. It takes me so much by surprise that I don't have time to react before she's on her feet and heading inside.

I touch my lips. That felt good. Too good.

18

———

Rose

God, I'm getting so many mixed signals from Aiden. He frowns while he pulls me close, pushes me away with an enticing smile. It's one hand saying no while tugging me back with the other. Kissing him was impulsive. I honestly didn't think about it beforehand. It just felt right. He's sweeter than I ever knew, and if anything, I'm falling for him harder, the more I know about him.

My head would spin if it weren't already going around from being so close to him. The scent of him, warm male skin and soap, makes me lightheaded with want. I want to bury my nose in the crease of his neck and stay there until the scent is old and boring. Like that could ever happen. I've never gotten sick of the scent of fresh-baked bread, so I don't think I could tire of Aiden's.

I'm wet down there. And I'm well aware of that fact when I feel my thighs slick together as I scurry back inside the cabin. I should shower and dress before I dive into work. And at some point today, I need to check in with Ing. For one, she'd kill me if she found out I kissed the Commander and didn't tell her immediately. It will have to be via text, obviously. I'm certainly not going to risk Aiden overhearing any conversations about him. I've fed his ego more than enough as it is.

I make myself go up the ladder to get fresh clothes — mine, this time. Everything aches as I pull myself up, but not in a scary way, so I know I'll recover, eventually. I'm lucky getting scraped up is all that happened.

I rethink that feeling of being okay when I'm in the shower and the hot water hits all my scratches and bruises. I immediately lower the water temperature, which helps, but I'm still hurting when I turn it off and get out. I towel off as gently as I can manage and then brave a look in the mirror. Fuck. I'm a mess. My body looks like it went through a blackberry thicket backwards. Okay, that would probably be even worse, but this is not attractive. If Aiden can get hard looking at me like this, he is either seriously twisted or really into me. Way more than he's letting on. Huh.

I swear I'm not doing this to be a tease, but I might as well have him check my back again before I get dressed. And if I wait, the anticipation of feeling his hands on me will kill me, so there's that. I wrap the large towel around me in a way that I can loosen it without flashing him and head out into the main room.

Someone groans from over at the dining room table, and I do my best to hide my smile. I pad over and turn my back to him. "Will you check it before I get dressed?"

"Yeah, that's probably a good idea." He doesn't sound too onboard, I have to say. But his hands gently tug on the towel so I loosen it in front until he has it down where he wants it and then hold the ends up over my breasts. His hands are warm, his fingers soft against my skin as he maps my back from top to bottom.

"Just a sec, I need the tweezers." He gets up and walks rather stiffly to the bathroom. My brain is taking in all the information and processing. It has yet to spit out a conclusion, probably because I'm afraid to hope.

Aiden comes back and sits down behind me. This time things hurt a little bit as he pinches my skin to maneuver some of the splinters out. "Sorry." He mutters after a particularly bad one.

"Beats getting an infection," I respond as cheerfully as I can manage.

"Much as I hate to say this, we should do this again tomorrow."

I nod jerkily. He can't see them from where he's sitting, but my nipples are proudly saluting against the terry cloth of the towel and it's all I can do not to arch my back and press my ass back against him. Yeah, not being that woman. Not yet, anyway.

I smile at him over my shoulder as I pull the towel up. "Thanks, Aiden."

He nods, frowning slightly. "Go get dressed."

I want to say something snarky like I always write love scenes naked (I don't, it's usually in pajamas with a large glass of wine). But I hold it in and head back into the bathroom. I have writing to do, words bubbling on my fingertips. I need to get them out and find out if they're usable. Confronting whatever is brewing with Aiden can wait. At least until after lunch.

I groan when I try to put on my bra. I won't be able to concentrate with the way the band rubs on my back, so I leave it off and get dressed in my jeans and the loosest of the tops that I brought. Something tells me Aiden will not look up from his reading unless he has to, so it shouldn't matter too much.

My desk is waiting for me patiently as I sit down and open up my laptop. At some point, before I talk to Aiden about what might be, I need to really think about what I want. A one-sided crush isn't even really comparable to a relationship. So do I want that with Aiden? Do I want to have to remember to not dump my frustrations on him when he walks in the door from a hard day in surgery?

I imagine that scene (yes, I should be writing something different right now). He'd be looking tired around the eyes, kind of like he does right now, maybe give me a half-smile. Would I be the fifties housewife that either meets him with a hard drink at the door or naked? No, that's not me. Never mind being from a different generation, it's not my personality.

No, I'd tell him knock-knock jokes until he switched his irritation from whatever had happened to me. Then I'd strip. Or let him spank me. I've never gotten off on that particular kink before but thinking of Aiden's large hand landing on my ass, um yes, please. (Okay, now I can't sit still.) Whatever.

19

Aiden

I can acknowledge when I'm wrong. I don't enjoy it any more than the next person, but I can manage it without pouting. I thought I made Rose come up here (never mind that she said she planned to anyway) so that she'd grow out of whatever fascination she had for me. And so I could supervise that process. If I were being brutally honest, I was planning to help her grow up a little.

I'm paying the price for my arrogance. And it's a very uncomfortable process. I'm flattered that Rose clearly hasn't lumped me in the old man camp, at least she seems to want to be around me. She kissed me like she was comfortable with me, not like she was trying to seduce me, which I find all the more tantalizing. Now I can't seem to stop myself from falling under her spell fast and hard. She *isn't* a little girl.

So where does that leave me? Where does that leave all the reasons I carefully listed out for not even considering the possibility of *something*?

Fuck if I know. I can't ever remember being this torn up about a woman before in my life. For the most part, sex either happened, or it didn't. I can't recall a single time worrying about it beforehand or feeling guilty after. Yes, my divorce was messy and we're definitely not friends, but sex wasn't part of the problem. Her being more interested in designer shoes than having a conversation with me definitely was.

Watching Rose over there typing away, biting her plump lower lip in frustration as her fingers fail to keep up with her brain, I can tell she works really hard. She'd have to, to finish a degree while writing twenty books. I don't know what she's done with the money, but it didn't go on clothes or shoes. I'll be impressed if it's all in savings and invested, but Rose is a little too softhearted for that. She's spent a bit of it, I'd be willing to bet on other people.

And shoot me, now I'm wondering how much sexual experience she's really had. I don't recall any mention of a serious boyfriend. If one had been on the horizon Tris would have gotten too anxious not to mention it. Rose will always be his little girl and without Monica to settle him down, his protective instincts largely go unchecked. Although Rose seems to know how to get her own way with him. So if her college years were anything like mine, people have been doing a lot of things without attaching a relationship label to it or telling Mom and Dad. God only knows what kids get up to these days.

It's highly unlikely she's a virgin. She's beautiful, funny, and smart. She was probably tripping over boys' tongues every time she left the house. But the sex scenes she writes aren't even physically possible a lot of the time. I know she's not writing textbooks but… Damn it. Now that's all I can think about. Fuck immunization rates among the rural poor. Okay, I don't really mean that. That's important stuff. But my cock has zero interest in the transmission of measles and a rather deep fascination in introducing Rose to what a grown man can do that eager boys can't.

I force myself back to the medical journals for a while. Until I watch Rose walk across the floor headed for the kitchen with an empty mug in her hand. This should not be erotic under any scenario. But watching the bob and sway of her breasts under her cotton shirt, I can barely breathe. I clear my throat, trying to get air down the passageway, and Rose swings her gaze to me.

She smiles slightly, "Hey, how's the reading going?"

"Slowly. How's the writing?"

"I'm on fire. Thanks for the inspiration." She grins, "One way or another you seem to get me writing. Maybe I need to keep you around." She keeps going into the small kitchen area and I'm sitting here like a teenage boy whose swimsuit model fantasy just showed up at his bedroom door. I should probably just acknowledge at this point that women are really the ones in charge, even when they're twenty years younger.

Rose and I need to talk bluntly about this thing between us before it blows up with unintended consequences. Particularly since it seems to be growing instead of dissipating. But I don't want to interrupt her writing. I know that she needs to get this book done so I simply watch her, brooding about all the reasons this is not a good idea until it's time for lunch.

For once, I don't give a damn about being healthy and pull out a frozen pizza that's loaded with extra cheese. By the time the oven is hot and I'm sliding it in, Rose is standing by her computer stretching her arms over her head and doing some weird-ass yoga poses.

"Ten-minute warning," I call to her.

"Got it." She smiles at me upside down and I shake my head. I need to get out and stretch my muscles too, if I'm honest. A solid run down the mountain and back up might focus some of my energy in a better direction. Maybe I just need some distance from Rose to regain my perspective. Yeah right, my cock is practically laughing at me. Distance is only going to make me run back faster, and a part of me knows it. She's a magnet for all my focus. Something my cock hasn't even tried to hide. The rest of me is still resisting, but surrender is approaching fast.

20

Rose

When Aiden puts the mathematically sliced pizza on the table with a frown, I know something's on his mind. More than was keeping him preoccupied before.

I'm feeling good about the words I've put on the page so far, so I hope he's not going to mess with my muse. I've lost a lot of time so I'm not out of the woods yet, but I've got the bones of a good story. The hero isn't Aiden in any shape or form, but he's still an alpha good guy and I genuinely like him. I made him a cop (with a trust fund since everyone is expecting more billionaires) who rescues a feisty damsel in distress (car trouble) and arrests her so he can keep her in town long enough to make his case.

The fact that I'm rooting for him makes writing so much easier. I want him to be happy so I'll cheerfully put in the work until he gets his girl who is super smart, extra hot, and perfect for him in every way (of course)!

I sit down and grab a slice of pizza. I'm a little surprised that Aiden didn't even add vegetables to the toppings. Has he given up worrying about both our sets of arteries? I doubt it. Guess I'll enjoy the cheese while it lasts. He'll probably come to his senses and make something uber healthy for dinner, lentils, or something equally blech.

"After lunch, I'm going to go for a run. Then you and I should talk." His face isn't giving anything away and his tone is dead even.

I watch him while I reel in a dangling string of cheese as gracefully as possible. I'm so not that girl and it never bothered me before today. "Care to give me a hint?" I ask casually once my mouth isn't full.

He only quirks an eyebrow at me. "Elephants," he says dryly, and I burst out laughing.

"Okay." I shrug. There's not much point in avoiding it. I mean we could go fuck and talk about it after or we can talk and then go fuck. I'm proud of my positive thinking there, no 'or' just 'and'. In any event, dancing around it the last couple of days hasn't made it go away, so maybe I can have a call with Ing after all if he's going to be out of the house. I could really use her input before things progress much further. I'm in uncharted territory here. Neither of us thought our fantasies would ever even shake hands with reality.

"How far are you running?"

I see his lips quirk and realize how my question could be interpreted, but he stays away from the danger zone, "Down the mountain and back."

"You're going to run *up* the mountain?" The same grade that made poor Kevin's engine practically choke, which reminds me that my car is still sitting down at the shopping center.

Aiden grins, "Don't clock me please but yes, that's the plan."

I want to tell him not to overdo it, to take his phone with

him, but I don't think fussing is going to help right now. "You could run down and then drive my car back up?" I ask hopefully. I'm not really looking forward to going back for it, but I'll need to retrieve Kevin relatively soon before someone steals him if they haven't already.

"You're right, that's a good idea. I don't really want you down there again. Give me your keys and I'll bring it back."

"Thanks," I sag with relief, even though I should put on my big girl panties and deal with a problem I created for myself. "His name is Kevin, and he doesn't like the steep grade very much, so go easy on him, okay?"

"You named your car, Kevin?" His voice is filled with disbelief.

"Yes. It suits him. He's very steady and reliable. Most Kevins are, in my experience."

Aiden's eyes are narrowing, he looks a little pissed off although why I have no idea. Old Hondas aren't usually the stuff to incite grand passions.

"So why did you pick that tattoo?" I ask as casually as I can manage, then stuff my mouth again. I'm partly trying to changing the subject, but also I really want to know. I always have ever since the first time I saw it.

Aiden chokes, then mutters 'fuck,' before answering, "It was all a mistake of youthful foolishness. Which should be a lesson to you, young Rose."

I roll my eyes, "I'm listening, oh wise old one. What's the scoop?"

"Nothing to be proud of. It was supposed to be a snarling tiger."

I snort-laugh, "Seriously?"

"I was nineteen, Rose. Drunk *and* stupid." His tone is self-deprecating, but his eyes are smiling as he slides one more slice of pizza onto his plate.

"Okay, so you went in and asked for a tiger, then what happened?"

"We were in Thailand. The guy claimed not to speak English, but in retrospect, I think he was just messing with us. So I found a website with a picture of what I wanted and pointed to it. The guy nodded, and the tiger is not what I got." He shrugs like it's no big deal.

"Wow. Well, if it helps, what you have probably *is* better than a tiger."

"Water under the bridge, either way."

We finish eating companionably in relative silence. I guess both of us have a lot on our minds. I wonder if any of the elephants will have heart-shaped polka dots. Yeah, probably not.

Aiden takes my car keys when I hand them to him and heads out the door, dressed in high-end running gear. It's not super tight, but he looks ready to attack one of those survival long-distance races and it makes me go weak in the knees. I wait until I know he's well out of hearing distance, and then I grab my phone and frantically call Ing. She picks up instantly.

"Rosey? I've been worried about you. What's going on?"

"Um, it's good, I think. The Commander and I are holed up in my dad's cabin."

"What!?" She screeches. "Together? Oh, my God. Did you sleep with him? Did he take your v-card finally? I'm going to faint with excitement."

"Wait on that," I laugh. "No, I slept with him, but it was only sleep. I didn't have sex with him. Yet."

"Yet? What does that mean?" She's practically screaming with excitement.

"It means there are all kinds of sexual tension flying and he wants to talk when he gets back from his run. Which is why I'm calling you now. Well, and I really wanted to check-in and make sure *you* are okay."

"Hmmm, Don't change the subject, missy. Do you want to sleep with him? Fuck him? Whatever?"

"Yeah, I really do," I answer softly.

"Well, just be careful then. It's not like he's a stranger at a bar, right?" I shudder. I don't want to get into that with Ing. She'll worry, and there's nothing she can do, anyway.

"I think I'm falling in love with him for real, Ing."

"Oh, sweetie. That's going to hurt. Big time."

"I know." God, we're both such dramatic pessimists. I don't know why I can't picture happily ever after with Aiden, but just a short, amazing fling. Maybe because my heart is afraid to hope. Maybe because I lost my mom so young. I'm sure a shrink would be happy to inform me of many more possibilities, but it comes down to I think it's worth it, anyway. For Aiden to be my first, probably my only for a long time to come, anyway. At least I'll know what it's like to have him focus on me as a woman, and I'll have memories to look back on instead of my rather fertile imagination. This is one of the rare times when I'm confident that reality is going to be so much better.

"So tell me about you. Where are you right now?"

"I'm in Arkansas. I'm out in the diamond field right now. Can you believe it?"

"Oh, my God. Did you find any yet?"

"Just a couple of tiny specks yesterday. Tomorrow is my last day here, and then I'm planning to drive straight through to North Carolina. Or at least this is my last major stop. I'm not stupid enough to drive through the night."

"You'll find a big one I just know it," I tell her, thinking positive thoughts in her direction. She's been talking about going to the Crater of Diamonds State Park ever since she saw it on TV a couple of years ago. We'd planned to go together, but well, Darla happened. Darla has a lot to answer for, both in the good and bad columns of my life.

"Anything from Justin?" I ask quietly, as if I'm afraid of conjuring him up in front of her.

"Nooo. Not exactly. I saw a strange man at a rest stop the day before I got here, and then again yesterday after I got to the park. Could be just a coincidence, of course. Or it might be one of his PIs."

"Or a freakin' serial killer! Be careful, Ing. Don't be out alone and make sure you barricade your hotel room."

"I'm being careful. And I've got mace on me. If I see him after I leave here, I'll do something. I don't know what though." She adds doubtfully.

"Did you check your car for trackers? That's how they always follow people on TV."

She laughs, "Um, what would I be looking for, exactly?"

"I'm not sure but maybe look around for something small that doesn't look like it should be there? Or better yet, switch cars. Ditch yours there and hire a rental. I'll pay for it." I'm actually working myself up into being seriously worried for her.

"That's not a horrible idea, Rose. I'll look into it. I hate to abandon Bob like that, but at least it's warm here. He wouldn't die of rust shame like he would up north."

I snicker, "If it helps, I don't think I'll be keeping Kevin around past this summer either. Remember what we agreed? Time to move on."

"Ha! Looks like you're moving straight into his bed, babe. You owe me all the details, by the way."

"Highlights. I will commit to highlights only." I mock sternly.

"Guess it is serious then, isn't it?" Her soft answer makes me think and yearn. I want him back here now so we can talk about those damn elephants.

"Yeah. Call me if you need me to transfer a deposit or whatever for the car. You know I'm good for it."

"I think I can manage this part, but I'll let you know what happens. Cheers, Rose."

And we hang up.

21

Aiden

I'm running like my conscience is chasing me. And maybe it is. But I'm getting to the point where I just don't care anymore. I would never deliberately hurt Rose. At the same time, I can't keep my hands off of her for much longer. Seeing her beautiful skin scratched and hurting, I want to kiss every inch until she feels worshipped like a goddess.

How crazy is it that now I sound like one of her books? Maybe reading all that silly romance stuff rubbed off on my subconscious. In which case this run should purge it from my system, not make me think about her even more.

I slow down as I hit a series of switchbacks. The last thing I need to do now is twist a knee or ankle. It's beautiful out here under the trees, not a soul around, just a few curious chipmunks staring at me. Birds are singing as they go about their daily business. By the time I reach the base of the mountain, I'm feeling pleasantly stretched and more energized than when I left the cabin. But all I can think about is getting back to Rose, finally talking through this *thing* and figuring out what to do about it together.

I still have to retrieve her car though, and that's another fifteen-minute walk. When I arrive at the shopping center, it looks perfectly ordinary. I see her car parked in a row with others, and it's as if nothing ever happened. I shake my head. There's nothing more I can do about the situation, really. The cops know. They've got the bad guy and Rose seems to be doing okay. I slide her keys out of my thigh pocket and go to her vehicle. It takes me a minute to get the seat back as far as it will go. Even then it's an extremely uncomfortable fit, but I can suffer through it for a few more minutes. I pull out and drive down the road towards the one that will lead back up the mountain.

Rose was right. Her car is on its last legs based on how it's responding to this hill. But it makes it, barely. I frown down at the gauges. I'm not happy about her driving this alone anywhere. It's too likely to break down either in the woods or on the freeway. But since I don't think she needs to go anywhere for at least the next three weeks, I'll table that argument for later.

When I enter the cabin, she's back in front of her computer, typing away. I'm not sure if she even registers my presence but I need a shower before we talk anyway so I head into my room to grab clean clothes. When I turn, she's in the doorway.

"Hey, everything go okay?"

"Yeah, your car is out front. I'm going to grab a shower and then we'll talk, okay?"

She nods, biting her lip. I drop a soft kiss on her forehead, "Stop worrying. We'll figure something out."

"I'm not worried. Just… anxious, I guess."

Now I'm the one frowning. What the heck does she have to be anxious about? I sigh and grab my clothes. Shower first, talk later.

Rose

I don't know what I was expecting. But it wasn't Aiden striding out of the bathroom, his dark hair still wet from the shower and *stalking* towards me like I'm all he can see. Without blinking, he picks me up from where I'm standing, stationed in front of the big windows overlooking the hillside, and carries me over to the kitchen counter.

Then, still without saying a word, he steps between my legs and kisses me, just like one of my book's heroes. I mean, he was all in. In ways I never dared imagine. His lips ground against mine, his tongue pushing at the seam until I allowed him entrance. Then he claimed my mouth, letting me know in no uncertain terms that he knew how to kiss a woman with utmost skill and that he was completely in charge of the situation.

I decided to enjoy the moment because all too soon he would step back, like he's doing now. He holds my chin gently in one hand, not letting me hide while his blue eyes, the color of the sea on a blustery day, search mine. I have no idea what he's looking for. "I thought we were going to talk," I say simply.

"That was talking. You had a lot to say, some of it I knew and some of it surprises me." He lowers his hand and uses both to grip my hips firmly.

I like, no, I love having his hands on me. There's something about him that my body and soul recognize. I can't really find the words to explain it. Just that when my hands rest on his shoulders, I can't imagine anyone else's shoulders ever feeling so *right*. Or another man's hands, simply placed on my hips, not moving, making me feel heat spreading through my core until I'm twitching with a need to get closer to the source.

"What did I say exactly?" And how much damage control do I need to do? I'm asking silently.

"That there's nothing artificial about you. You aren't trying to prove a point, or cover up for some insecurity. That you like me kissing you." He frowns slightly, "And that you don't have nearly as much experience as your writing would suggest."

I blush, I know I do. Fuck. I've never been embarrassed or ashamed by my lack of experience. It was completely my choice. I chose not to play around at frat parties to 'experiment' as my peers would say. Not because I'm a prude, but because I knew the experience would be empty compared to what it could be if I had feelings for someone. Someone like Aiden. But now I'm wondering if that was the wrong approach. Should I have practiced with someone equally young and foolish, learned a few skills?

"I really don't like where your thoughts are going, Rosebud." Aiden's voice is laced with exacerbation.

"What do you think I'm thinking?" I'm even more chagrined that he can read me like a book. If he really can, that is.

"You're wishing you had fooled around more than you had, so I wouldn't be able to tell your lack of experience. And I'm telling you that your... openness is charming. It's intoxicating. But I do need to ask exactly how far you've gone."

Fuck. I try to hide my face against his chest, but he won't let me. His arms have come up to hold me at the shoulders and he braces them to keep the space open between us.

"Would you ask any other woman that question right now, Aiden?"

"You aren't any other woman, Rosebud. You're my best friend's daughter, which makes this wrong on so many levels. You're also so right I can't force myself to walk away. Which is not *any other woman*. So we're going to stay here until you break it down for me."

"Um." I focus my gaze on his lips. I can't look into his eyes right now. They're too overwhelming. "Not really any. I mean, I kissed a boy in high school once. At a dance. That's about it."

I hear his ragged intake of breath that exhales with, "Fuck." But I still can't meet his gaze. I place my palms on his chest, needing that contact, that connection with him, and am soothed by the steady beat of his heart.

"So nobody has ever sucked those pretty nipples?"

I shake my head no.

"Or even fingered your virgin pussy?"

Again, I indicate no.

"And you want me to do that to you?"

I nod, a tiny smile curving my lips. "And…"

"And what?" He's patiently waiting. Not tugging at me or barking orders for once.

"I want you inside me, Aiden. I need to know all of you."

He groans and pulls me closer where I can finally plaster myself against him, "You are going to be the death of me, Rosebud. I'm done trying to deny that I'm attracted to you. No, that makes it sound mild and pleasant. I think I'm becoming obsessed with you. But we need to take this slow for both our sakes. So I'm not going to fuck you."

"What?!" I push back so I can glare at him in disappointment.

He chuckles, but the laughter doesn't quite meet his eyes, "Relax little one, I didn't say we weren't going to do other stuff. You'll sleep in my arms every night and I'm going to show you what a man can make you feel without stuffing his cock in your adorable little pussy. You and me being together isn't as simple as one of your books, Rosebud."

"Why not?" I pout. I want all of him. Before he wakes up and decides he doesn't want any of me.

"For starters, what would you tell your dad? What would you say to your friends? Are you really prepared to tie yourself to a middle-aged man living in a small town in rural Washington?"

I straighten my spine. "I'm willing to figure those things

out. I don't think anyone of any age can answer that without being able to tell the future. That's what dating is for."

"You're right, but that's kind of my point. How would you and I date? We don't even live in the same place."

Okay, I see his point, but that hasn't stopped me from wanting him for the last seven years. "Aiden, just remember that I've had these feelings for you longer than you've thought that way about me. Perfectly understandable under the circumstances, but please try to not be condescending."

"That's fair, but my rule applies. If you leave here a technical virgin, I won't feel I've stolen something from you unfairly."

I sigh. He's splitting hairs, but if it makes him feel better, I can argue my point later. "Fine. Are you going to kiss me again, then?"

He smacks me on the lips all too briefly, "Not more than that, no. I need to get dinner started and you have some more writing to do, I believe. We'll revisit your new lessons tonight."

Oh God, my pussy is clenching with anticipation. And suddenly I'm not sure I can survive without touching him. I let my hands linger around his neck as he lifts me down. His skin is damp from the shower but oh so warm and he smells of... I don't know... is there such a thing as a clean alpha male smell? If there is, that's what Aiden smells like right now. I don't want to walk away from that scent. It's too intoxicating.

Reluctantly I go back to my computer, but as soon as I sit down the words spill off my fingers. Aiden has to call me twice before I hear him tell me dinner is ready.

22

———

Rose

Looks like we're back to extreme healthy eating. Not a shred of cheese anywhere on the table, but I have to admit the chicken curry over brown rice smells amazing. I suddenly realize I'm starving, but that doesn't stop me from watching Aiden's hands as he eats. He has surgeon's hands, there's no doubt about that. Long, dexterous fingers that have me transfixed.

"Darling Rose, you are dangerously good for my ego."

"Hmmm?" I bring my eyes up to find him smirking at me. I shrug. Now that we've reached some kind of... I'm not sure what — Agreement? Compromise? — I decide I get to drink him in without shame.

"Eat, Rosebud. I have plans for you later."

"How much later?" I don't want to be half-asleep and miss the good parts.

He laughs, his face more open than I've seen since I got here, and it makes my heart leap in my chest.

"You still get to do the dishes while I make a fire. The rest is to be… explored together, I'd say."

I swallow hard.

Aiden's voice softens, "Rose, you can change your mind at any time. I will absolutely not hold it against you."

"I'm more worried about you changing yours," I admit, daring to meet his gaze head-on.

"That's why I set some guardrails in place. Things not moving forward past a certain point will never be because I don't want you enough."

And I don't know why I needed to hear that, but I did. I go back to eating my dinner thoughtfully. He's right, this is more than just tonight and it's not a fairy tale. No matter how much it feels like one in the moment. We finish and I stand up to gather our plates. A few minutes alone in the kitchen with the prosaic task of washing up suits me just fine.

As I wash, I hear Aiden going about making a fire in the bright blue-enameled wood stove. After I place the last dish in the drainer, I dry my hands on a towel and turn.

He's spread a soft blanket out in front of the cheerful stove along with a few pillows. He's lounging there with his back against the couch, staring into the flames.

"Aiden?"

He looks up with a wry smile, "Come here, Rose. If you dare."

I'm drawn to him like a moth to the flame, and he tugs me down onto his lap. I melt into him, pulling his mouth down to mine. He indulges me, I'm sure of it. Would a more sophisticated woman, the kind he's probably used to, simply undress and take his cock in her mouth? I don't know. I'm not her and he knows that.

So he kisses me. Soft slow kisses and hard, punishing kisses that melt into butterfly touches along my throat. I lose my ability to think, caught up in the current of his touch.

Then he's pulling my t-shirt over my head. He shifts me on his lap until he can bend down to take my erect nipple into his mouth. He bathes it with his tongue, then bites with just enough pressure for me to feel it right down to my toes, which curl in response. "Aiden!"

"So responsive, Rosebud. Tell me what you want." His dark head comes up to kiss the corner of my mouth. I turn my head to align our lips, but he leans back.

"More. I want more." I try to pull his head down again.

"And you'll get it. But since I'm the one with experience here, can we agree that I'm in charge?"

I don't answer, I'm too busy trying to merge my body with his.

"Rose? I need you to say it."

"Fuck! Fine, you're in charge."

He's laughing, "Was that so hard? I need you out of your jeans and panties now."

I don't bother questioning that. If it will get his mouth on me that much faster, I'm all for it. I shimmy out of my jeans and he helps pull them from my legs.

Now I'm naked and he's still dressed. "But what about…?"

He points to his chest, "In charge, remember? You seem to have some difficulty letting go of control."

He looks around and then leans over to grab a pillow off the couch. "Lie down with your head on the cushion."

I do as he asks, feeling the heat from the fire on my bare skin.

"Now reach your hands up and grab the corners."

"Why?"

"Because I said so." He waits until I do as he asked. I want to touch him so it's with reluctance that I bring my hands up. When I have, he adds, "If you bring your hands down, I'll assume you want to stop."

"But…"

He raises an eyebrow, "Hands up we continue, hands down, we stop."

I nod because I don't think I have a choice, not if I'm going to get what I want.

"Good girl."

I've typed that phrase a million times I swear and never once did it make me as wet as I am now. "Aiden!"

"Patience, Rosebud. Your pleasure is not something to be rushed."

I'd be fine with rushing it a little, really I would, but it's clear he has a plan he's following like a military drill. God help me.

Aiden

Rose looks like a primeval Celtic goddess spread out before me. Her red hair catches the light from the fire and seems to blaze with a heat of its own. Her blue eyes, usually sparkling with humor even when she's anxious, are smoky with desire. I want her to feel the way I see her, as a glorious young woman with the world ready to bow at her feet.

That doesn't mean I'm not going to enjoy winding her up until she thinks she can't take any more. With her hands up by her head, her breasts rise unencumbered, begging for my attention. I kneel between Rose's splayed legs and bend down to savor her tits. I test her responses for slow, soft, and more punishing touch. She seems to like it a little rough, which surprises me, although I'm not sure why. She's not acting. Every response seems to catch her by surprise, and I feel blessed by the gods to be the man who witnesses that.

When she's biting her lip and I feel her legs moving restlessly against my hips, I leave her breasts (reluctantly) and move down to her pussy. Sliding one finger down her seam, she's dripping wet. "That all for me, Rosebud?"

She half laughs, half groans, "Do you see anyone else here?"

I growl and nip her hip with my teeth in warning, "You're mine, Rose. Fully and completely."

"Yes." She acknowledges as if I'm simply stating a basic truth and not staking a claim.

I part her folds with my fingers and dive in. Her taste is divine. Delicate honey with a hint of citrus, she's intoxicating. My tongue pushes into her virgin channel and I hear her gurgle in response. I check to see if she's obeyed my instructions. Her hands are still on the cushion. Good. I return to savor her pussy, licking up her seam to suck gently on her hard little bud.

"Aiden!" She practically levitates off the floor. I wait for her to come down again. "Hands, Rose." Instantly she reaches for the pillow behind her head, but that doesn't stop her dramatic eye-rolling. I grin and tease her clit, circling around it with my finger without touching the nub itself, watching it swell and change color in fascination.

She's whimpering now, and this has probably been enough for our first lesson. So I slide one finger into her pussy, watching as her face changes with the invasion.

"How does that feel, Rose?"

"Good, so good. I want more."

A second finger joins the first, and she sighs in satisfaction. As I pump my fingers in and out, curling them ever so slightly, I take her clit into my mouth again. Sucking lightly and then with more force, I move my fingers as I feel her climax gathering, swirling into a storm of epic proportions. When I scrape my teeth gently over her, she falls apart, screaming with release. Her pussy tightens over my fingers, making my cock ache with anticipation of how she would grip my girth. I continue to move my hand in and out of her, gentling her as she comes down, her limbs going from full tension to utter boneless relaxation.

I move back up her body, taking her lips with mine, letting her taste herself on me. She opens for my tongue like she was waiting for it.

"Come on, sweet Rose. Time for bed."

"I don't think I can move."

I smile, she's adorable and despite my rigid cock that will see no relief tonight I can't wait to hold her in my arms. I help her up, admiring the long lines of her body as she leans against me. Then I pick her up and carry her into the bedroom. When I have her tucked under the covers, I make sure the cabin is secure and the fire safe for the night. Then I strip and crawl into bed. Rose flows into my arms like water.

"You didn't…" She asks softly.

"Tomorrow you can taste my cock if you want to. Sleep now, Rosebud."

She presses a soft kiss to my shoulder and then I'm pretty sure she's out like a light.

23

Rose

I wake to find myself wrapped around Aiden like a pretzel. I can feel his cock, large and hard, pressing against my stomach. I know how men feel about clingy women so I try to move away but Aiden pulls me tight against him, his arms steel bands holding me close.

"Morning, Rosebud."

"Um. Good morning. Aren't you… um…"

"What?"

"Um. In pain?"

"More like anticipation. You ready for that next lesson?"

Oh my God, really? Before I've even brushed my teeth? "Um, sure?"

He chuckles against my ear. "Relax. Nothing you can't handle this morning. As long as you don't mind getting a little messy. But then you're a bit of a dirty girl, aren't you? I've read your books after all."

"Uh, that was mostly my imagination, but okay. What did you have in mind?"

"I'll make you cum with my fingers and then I'll show you how to touch a man's cock. I'm going to cum all over your pretty pale skin, possibly rub it in so you always remember who you belong to. Then we can shower."

"Together?" I squeak, it's more about the visual he's just um, painted, than the idea of showering together.

"Um-hmm. I'm ready to get my mouth on your sweet pussy again."

"O-o-okay." It's still dark out, so this conversation is happening without being able to look in his eyes. I have to say, Aiden is seriously good at dirty talk and I'm eating it up with a spoon.

"Such a good girl," he purrs in my ear and I shudder, which makes him laugh.

His hand reaches between my legs, which open to his touch like they recognize who's in charge. I'm languid and sleepy, but it only takes a few swipes of his finger to have my body jerking in his arms, my pussy spasming around his talented fingers.

When I can breathe somewhat normally again, Aiden rolls to his side, guiding my hand onto his cock, showing me how to touch him in long smooth strokes. "But first, you need some lube."

"Um."

"Your own will do, sweet Rose." He takes my hand and rubs my fingers against my pussy which is still soaking wet, then he brings my hand back to his cock and lets me find my way. I'm tentative at first. This is, after all, the first real cock I've ever touched, but his quickened breathing encourages me and before long I'm testing his endurance.

"Fuck, Rose." He groans and then he's shouting my name while long ropes of cum spray across my thighs and midriff.

He rises over me, and my legs instinctively open to cradle

his pelvis with mine. He sucks hard on the side of my neck while his hands do just as he promised, rubbing his cum into my skin. It's the most erotic thing ever. His cock is still half-hard sliding against my slit and I shift, trying to find the perfect alignment that will bring us together.

Aiden pulls back a little. Then kisses me deeply, his tongue claiming my mouth with authority. "Beautiful, Rose. You are perfection."

But still a virgin, I pout into the darkness. But I don't say anything.

He leans over and turns on the bedside light, then pulls the covers back to stare at me. I shiver but couldn't say if it was from the cold of the room or the heat in his gaze.

"Beautiful," he says with pride. "Come on. I'll warm you up in the shower."

What does that mean? I follow him naked and shivering into the bathroom.

It turns out it means having his face buried in my pussy once again while the hot water pounds onto my back and my legs tremble with release. When I can't possibly take anymore, Aiden washes me gently, dries me off, and then helps me dress.

He leaves me to dry my hair while he goes to make break-fast. He surprises me though when I go to sit down by pulling me down onto his lap. He feeds me bites from his plate until I turn my head away and bury it in his neck. We sit there for a while longer, his long fingers tracing the lines of my back while I breathe in his magnificent scent and try not to think about forever.

We fall into a pattern, Aiden and I, over the next few days. I wake far earlier than I would normally — usually to find his head between my thighs, licking me into oblivion. Then sometimes, he lets me return the favor. I take a curious pride in being able to make him lose control. Although he never completely lets go. He still refuses to 'go all the way' as kids say.

Then we shower, usually together, and I get more of a chance to explore his body. He still feels like my true other half, a fitter, more beautiful half. He's patient with my tentative touches, up to a point. And when we reach that moment, I find myself up against the shower stall impaled on his fingers until I cum to his satisfaction.

I'm exhausted (but very happy) by the time I sit down to write after breakfast. My novel is practically telling itself, and I know my writing is different. It's not the sexy parts, although those are probably more poetic. There's a different rhythm to the whole thing. A little more anxiety or uncertainty to the characters' relationship. I'm not a fool, I know I'm writing out my own fears.

Aiden never talks about the future, and it's bothering me. He doesn't discuss what he expects to happen or what he wants from me after we both leave the cabin. That deadline is now only two weeks away, and I realize something isn't quite right. But whenever he touches me, which is often unless I'm sitting in front of my computer, my doubts fly out the window and I flow into his embrace like I've always had that privilege.

I *love* being able to kiss him when I feel like it. I relish the time spent out on the deck, curled up on his lap while he makes love to me with his mouth and fingers as I watch the sunset. He claims he's watching it too, but every time I check I find his eyes are on me. I'm not really complaining.

Ing has texted me a few times to let me know she finally arrived in North Carolina. She loves her beach house and her new car, which is a ten-year-old Subaru that came with a roof rack for a surfboard. She's thinking about taking lessons just so she can use the damn rack.

I didn't tell her about the further developments with Aiden.

Not after that initial kiss. She asked once or twice, but I put her off. I think I was afraid of how small it would all look in words in a text message. Feelings are so much bigger.

I've hit the point in my book where the two main characters encounter their major conflict, the one that could split them up, permanently or temporarily. Naturally, the readers all know it's going to be temporary, but it still has to be there and be at least somewhat convincing. I'm finding it hard to bring the conflict to a conclusion. Maybe they don't belong together after all? Maybe the whole story is crap. I sigh and go to make myself a cup of tea. Only the cupboard is bare. I've used up all of Aiden's fancy herbal sachets or whatever the heck those things are.

"Aiden? Did you get any other kind of tea?" He doesn't answer, so I look around and realize he's not in the cabin. I double-check the cupboard again. No tea. It's not the end of the world, but now I'm curious where he is because he usually tells me if he's going out for a run or something. I put on my tennis shoes, the ones I use for walking in the woods, and head out the door with my phone in my pocket just in case.

I can hear the axe from half a mile away, although I find him in a clearing closer to the cabin than that. His shirt is off and he's splitting wood with his back to me. I stop and stare. First of all, because he's male poetry in motion. His muscles aren't all bunchy, but they're lean and smooth like a marble sculpture of a Roman warrior. And second, because anger and frustration are pouring out of him with every downward slice of the axe. What the hell?

I watch for a few more minutes and then retreat to the cabin. My brain is going a million miles an hour and none of the scenarios it comes up with are happy ones. If Aiden knew I was standing there watching him, he never let on. He seemed lost in whatever that was he was working out. I learned when my mom was sick that avoiding the things you know are going to hurt you doesn't make it hurt any less. It just adds anxiety on top of the pain, which makes everything worse.

So I go back to my writing and decide that these two characters will have the best dang happy-ever-after that could ever be found between two covers. (The bed or the book kind, it doesn't matter!) Because it's becoming increasingly clear to me that I'm not going to get that for myself. Not with Aiden. I'm mostly okay with that. I think. But I am impatient, and if I'm going to be crying my eyes out, I'd just as soon get it over with so I can pick myself up and move on.

24

Aiden

The guilt is eating me alive. Not for making love to Rose, because even though I haven't sunk my cock into her sweet body, that's what we're doing. With every thrust of my fingers, every caress of her hand against my cock, we're lovers. She's so incredibly giving and the most responsive woman I've ever been with. I swear she could cum just from me looking at her a certain way. And doesn't that make me feel like I own the world?

I cherish every moan and spasm she gives me. Each one filed away in my memory for that time when she's no longer here.

No, I'm beating myself up for what I'm taking from her by tying her to me. A family of her own, a chance to have kids, make Tris a proud grandpa.

Even if I wanted kids, which I can't even imagine, I don't picture my best friend doing anything but cringing if I fathered his daughter's children. That's not entirely fair because he's the kind of pediatrician that really enjoys being around kids and never once blames them for their parents' mistakes. But still.

And I'm committed for at least the next five years to the hospital in Destiny Bay, a rural area in upstate Washington, hours from the nearest real shopping mall. I know Rose doesn't mind roughing it for a week or two, but what woman doesn't want to go hunting for shoes and hitting the spa up on a weekly basis? Particularly if she can afford to, which I'm guessing Rose can.

She's mentioned a little more about her publishing business over the last few days, and she definitely doesn't need me to take care of her financially. Hell, she might just make more than I do this year. I'm proud of her but a little at a loss as to how I'm possibly a check mark in the positive column of her life. Beyond the sex, anyway.

And yet I can't seem to let her go. Not yet. I know she's wondering what I'm playing at, blowing hot and cold. She's smart and observant. I wish I knew why I can't make myself move in either direction. Either let her go or plan a future together. It's like they're evenly balanced options and I'm stuck in the middle bouncing between them.

I wish beyond words that I had a plan to offer that tied everything up with a nice neat bow and gave us both what we wanted. Bottom line: I don't trust that she's not still just going through a phase, still growing up. She's going to wake up any day now and realize she's better off with someone closer to her age. Someone that can adapt his life to her dreams. And he'd better. If any man ever tries to hold Rose back, I'll fucking kill him.

I want to kill this imaginary man I've paired her up with anyway for even thinking about touching *my* Rose. So yeah, I'm screwed and I know it.

So I'm out here splitting enough firewood to heat the cabin for three years, that's if Tris ever drags his sorry ass up here again, and trying to figure out how to let Rose go. I'm pretty sure she's worked her way so deep in my psyche pulling her away is going to leave a big raw gaping wound. Damned if I can see an alternative.

When my arms are aching so badly, they're trembling and I'm in real danger of sinking the axe in my foot, I stop chopping and head back to the cabin. I need a shower and then Rose and I are going to have to talk. Fuck.

Rose

When I get back inside, I'm a little too unsettled from seeing Aiden so worked up to write, so I do the thing that put twenty extra pounds on me when I was a teenager. And it took way too many trips to the gym in college to make it go away again, but whatever. Brownies. They fix everything. Okay, maybe not, but they help. And I know the best recipe by heart.

So I go about melting chocolate and stirring in enough butter and sugar to make him faint with horror. I grin despite my trepidation about what's to come at that thought. Good, more brownies for me if his body is a fancier temple than mine. I promise you it is. And if I'm being completely honest, I will worship at his alter any day of the week. Just not when I'm about to break up with him. Although don't you have to be in an actual relationship to break up?

In any event, the best of chocolaty goodness is in the oven and I've just set the timer on my phone when Aiden comes in. He looks completely beat and sweaty. I can smell him from the other side of the cabin and I'm worried because he doesn't smell bad *at all*. I'll bet he's ruined me for any other man ever and I'm going to die a virgin. I check the timer. I need those brownies *now*. But only ninety seconds have passed since I set it.

Aiden heads straight into the shower without even glancing in my direction, and I sigh. This is going to be epically bad. He comes out wearing only a towel wrapped around his waist a few minutes later. This time his eyes meet mine warily and he half-smiles.

"We need to talk." I beat him to the punchline and his jaw hangs open for a second as though he's shocked. But he nods and turns into the bedroom to get dressed. Before I mixed up the brownies, I moved my stuff back upstairs. It had slowly migrated downstairs over the last several days, but the sex has to stop now or I'll never pick myself up from the emotional puddle I'm about to fall in.

I know he noticed my clothes missing while he got dressed, but he doesn't say anything when he comes back into the main room. He's dressed in old worn jeans that fit his butt to perfection (he would blush if I told him that) and an ancient t-shirt that was probably black at some point and is now some weird shade of greenish-gray.

"Want a brownie? They'll be ready in about ten minutes." It's a peace offering and a delaying tactic, but I'm not surprised when he refuses.

"No thanks. So what did you want to talk about? I've got a few things to go over with you as well."

I roll my eyes. I'm willing to bet we have pretty similar agenda items, but he's never going to admit it. God forbid he ever admits I'm a mature adult.

"We've both avoided talking about what happens when we leave the cabin. I'm getting the feeling that you don't think we'll be together in the future, but I don't want to make assumptions about your feelings." I'm very careful to keep my tone even and not accusatory, but I admit to using air quotes around the word 'together'. I couldn't help it.

"Rose..." He closes his eyes briefly, as though he's got a script written on the back of his eyelids for how to let me down easy.

"Aiden, it's okay. I learned a long time ago that trying to hold on to someone who isn't in a place where they can be held, makes it harder on everyone. And it doesn't work, anyway."

"Rose, you know I wouldn't hurt you for the world." He's in my space, holding on to my upper arms with a firm grip.

"I know that. But I also know you aren't ready to let me in, not all the way."

"You're so fucking young, Rosebud." He says it with deep regret and I blink furiously. I will not cry in front of this man. For one, it will make him feel even worse about something he can't control. Is he being an idiot? Yes, of course, he is. But I love him and I don't want him hurting, not over something that's really all my fault, anyway.

"Yeah, well. I'm doing everything I can about that, but I think we have to go back to being... roommates for a few days. I'll finish the book soon, it's been going faster than usual."

He frowns like that wasn't what he expected to hear. "That's probably for the best." He lets go of me and steps back. My phone alarm goes off, so I silence it and busy myself taking the brownies out of the oven. They smell divine and the steam helps disguise my too wet eyes.

"So," I manage fairly cheerfully, "was there anything else on your list for this meeting or did I steal your thunder?"

He smiles slightly, "Nothing that can't wait. Don't eat all those in one go. I'm planning to start dinner in a few minutes. Stir-fry okay with you?"

And just like that, the fact that I've had his huge cock in my mouth is pushed behind both of us, never to be mentioned again.

I hold myself together while he fixes dinner, and we sit

down to eat it. He tries to introduce a few neutral topics and I do my best to respond but I'm distracted and our conversation dwindles quickly. I keep wondering if he's going to stay alone forever or if he'll eventually find a woman he thinks suits him better. (She won't of course, but he might *think* that.) I know he hasn't been a complete monk, a man doesn't know how to use his tongue like that without practice. Still, I think he deserves something more than casual hookups. What if he gets sick? Who's going to make sure he sees a doctor? (Because like most physicians, I'm sure he's a crappy patient.)

I want him to be happy. But I'm not quite generous enough to say I hope he'll find that with someone else. Not yet. Try me again in a month or two. Okay, maybe don't ask for a couple of years. Aiden's a lot to get over, even if I never truly had him.

25

Rose

I'm ruthless with myself. I channel all the energy I want to spend crying into writing. My sanity depends on getting this damn book done and removing myself from Aiden's magnetic orbit. He looks a little lost, but he hasn't said a single word about the abrupt change in our relationship. I've heard him sigh heavily a few times, but he always musters some kind of smile when I look over.

When I'm not writing, I'm doing dishes and laundry. Aiden has chopped and stacked firewood until he had to stop to build a new frame to hold it all. His biceps have gotten bigger because of it. But his eyes are sad, and I hate that I had anything to do with that. For the first time, I seriously regret the chain of events that led to Darla. I'm absolutely not sorry that I know what it feels like to have Aiden's mouth on my pussy or his cum spray across my body. That I will treasure until I'm old and gray, waiting out my golden years in a rocking chair. In fact, I think I'll take those memories out often when I hit that stage of life. What I regret is dragging him into something not of his own making. I know without a shadow of a doubt he never would have looked at me in any kind of sexual way if I hadn't planted the idea in his head. And yes, I know I didn't make him act on it, I'm not that stupid or that much of a seductress, but I still feel guilty. The sooner I can get out of his orbit, the easier this will be for both of us.

I don't let myself think about the possibility that maybe someday he'll come to his senses. The man has been single for years, he's smooth and good looking with a great career. He's had choices. *And probably more sophisticated women than you trying to change his mind.* The nasty little voice says in my head.

I just keep writing. And then I hit the editing stage. That's when I have to take a long walk in the woods to let the tears fall. I make myself stop when I reach the lake so that my eyes won't be completely puffy by the time I get back. Because it's all there in the book if you know where to look. The surprise (he likes me!), the passion (oh my God!), the doubt (he doesn't love me), and the sorrow (goodbye, Aiden). Of course, I've wrapped it all up with a fictional bow of a happy ending. The readers may sense something different, but I very much doubt they'll be able to put their finger on it. I don't know what Aiden will make of it. I'm not really that sure he'll bother to read it, even though he'd said he was going to. I'm not sure I care.

When I get back from my walk, Aiden has disappeared somewhere, and I dive into the editing. Most of it is fairly mindless, I'm not messing with the story, the real editors can do that. I'm fixing things like my bad habit of using 'however' whenever I can't think of how else to word a sentence. It's lazy and I know it, but it's easier to fix it at the end than pause as I'm writing out the plot.

I think I'll be able to wrap it up tomorrow first thing in the morning. I stand and stretch in all directions. Aiden just came in and went straight for the shower, so I guess I'll head upstairs and pack. I'll tell him I'm going tomorrow. Before I do that, though, I flip through the pictures on my phone. I have a handful of Aiden when I was still thinking there was a chance. He's not big on having his picture taken, so I had to sneak in a few when he wasn't quite so self-conscious. Like when he was cooking dinner. But as I flip through them, I see that there's always something that seems slightly off. Like he's not completely comfortable in his own skin. I frown and bite my lip. I need to ask him about this. I delay the packing and go to straighten up the kitchen. I never did the lunch dishes — I was in too much of a hurry to get the book done. So I tackle them now. But then Aiden comes in to prepare dinner. And it's not that big of a kitchen.

"Aiden, can I ask you something personal?"

He raises an eyebrow that basically says you've seen me naked, what kind of personal are we talking about? But all he says is, "Of course, Rosebud. What's on your mind?"

"I was looking back at some of the pictures I took of you last week," (dear God, was that only last week? This is like a soap opera) "and you looked uneasy. Is there anything I don't know about?"

He shrugs, "No to the last, and it's probably guilt. I kept hoping I'd see a path forward that would leave it behind, but I don't think that's even possible."

"Oh."

"Nothing for you to worry about, Rose. That's all on me."

"Why?"

"Older, supposed to be wiser?"

I roll my eyes. "Maybe if you put the weight of the world down for a bit, you'd find it lighter the next time you pick it up." I totally stole that from a greeting card.

"The military doesn't really operate on that kind of philoso-phy." He says dryly.

"Yes, it does. Or at least it operates on one of teamwork. It has to. If it were every man for himself, nothing would get done."

"Not dumping my shit on your shoulders, young Rose. No matter what."

I shrug. Well, at least I tried. And his answer explains the weirdness in the pictures. I finish the cleanup and leave him in the kitchen while I go back to my phone. After careful deliberation, I delete all but one, my favorite when he was holding me on his lap and I took a selfie of the two of us. His gaze was on me and I can at least see affection mingling with the guilt in that one.

26

Rose

The end I type, sighing heavily as my fingers blindly find the right keys.

It's over. Those words are unlikely to stay in the manuscript when it's published, but I need to write them down. To force my brain to let go. And I'm relieved, sort of. While my hopes and dreams of a future with Aiden are dashed, at least the self-inflicted torture is done too. Or will be by the end of the day. I still have to get through saying goodbye to him and actually driving away.

I hope my absence will make this easier on him too. When I see the conflicted emotions in his eyes: affection, pain, self-doubt, frustration — it makes me a little sick. I don't want him to be miserable. He loves me — a little. Just not enough to overcome everything else. He never tried to make me believe otherwise, which is why it's my own damn fault for falling so hard so fast. *Of course, I had something of a head start.* My internal voice is wry. I can still laugh at myself. That's good.

I'm going to go spend a few days with Ingrid, and then I'm thinking about making some serious long-term travel plans. I'm toying with an extended trip to the UK or maybe New Zealand. I don't have the energy right now for visiting a country where I can't speak the language. I should visit my dad before I leave, but I'm too emotional to see him right now. He'll know something's wrong and try to drag it out of me. I'm not ruining Aiden's friendship with Dad on top of everything else, although knowing Aiden he'll need some time before he lets the guilt go enough to see Dad. Like he has anything to feel guilty about.

I send the book file to Aiden's phone and go to find him. He's in the kitchen chopping vegetables with brisk efficiency. "Aiden?"

His smile is tired when he meets my eyes, "What's up, Rose?"

"The book is done. I sent a copy to your phone so you can read it when you're ready. I'm going to go pack and get out of your hair."

"Rose, you don't have to…"

I stop his words with a finger to his perfectly shaped lips, "Yeah, I do. It's better this way." I press a light kiss to his cheek, "I dragged you into whatever this is, which was never my intention. I'm sorry."

"I'm not." His blunt words catch me by surprise. I'm not sure what's coming next, but it's not going to be a significant plot twist. He's still chopping carrots. Not exactly an indicator of a forthcoming declaration of passion.

"Just because I wish things were different, doesn't mean I regret getting to know you as your own person. You're more than Tristan's daughter, Rosebud. You're smart and funny and sexier than you'll ever realize."

I must have made a face because his eyes crinkle at the corners. "It's true, Rose. More so because you don't see it."

He wipes his hands on a dishtowel and leans against the counter, a safe three feet away from me, "So what's next? Did you decide where you're going to live?"

I shake my head, "I think I'm going to travel for a while. Shake up my life a bit, make room for some new experiences."

His eyes narrow dangerously, "Stay safe, okay? Don't go off with strange men."

I roll my eyes, "I wasn't talking about that kind of experience, Aiden. I thought I might start with bungee jumping or something."

That doesn't seem to make him any happier, he's practically growling, "Rosebud, just promise you'll call me if you need help. I don't care what's happened or not happened between us, I'll always be there for you if you need me."

"Okay." I try to smile but I'm getting teary so I turn away. This is why I need to leave the country. If I don't, I'll find some goddamn excuse to see him again and I'll never get over this. I head up to the loft to finish packing up my shit.

"And you're staying for lunch!" he shouts after me. That makes me smile, as he probably intended.

It doesn't take very long at all to throw my things into my two duffle bags and pack my laptop carefully into my backpack. When I take them outside to load my car, it's already uncomfortably warm. I take a minute to roll the windows down so it won't be a blast furnace by the time I leave. Poor Kevin is getting old and they say the air conditioning is the first to go. His usually takes about twenty minutes before anything comes out that's cooler than the surrounding air.

When it's time to come home again, I'll probably need to think about buying a new car. I've hung onto Kevin out of loyalty, but perhaps life would be easier if I find something where everything works. I pat the dash in apology before shutting the door.

Time for lunch.

It's really hard to eat around a lump in your throat. I manage, but only because keeping my attention focused on the food means I'm not staring at Aiden trying to commit every one of his facial expressions to memory.

Saying goodbye is awkward, to say the least. I do the dishes for the last time, despite his protests that he will take it from here, and then I kiss him on the cheek and whisper, "Don't work too hard."

To which he replies, "Drive safe, Rosebud."

And that was that. Now I'm crying my eyes out as I drive Kevin down the mountain. That's not quite as dangerous as it sounds. For starters, I put the car in third gear as soon as I left the driveway and I'm not bawling so my eyes are open. I'm just having a cathartic cry. Partly because I'm not even sure where I'm headed. I want to go home to my dad and yet that's also the last place I want to be. I think I need those few days with Ing to decompress, but I don't have the patience to drive all the way to North Carolina. And I don't think Kevin would make it.

The cheapest and easiest thing to do is drive back to San Diego, find some long-term parking at the airport, and hit up the airline counter for the next available flight to Raleigh. I am of course making a huge assumption that Ing is willing to have a guest.

No way am I stopping at the San Sebastian shopping center again, so I keep driving until the rural road merges with the rural highway. Then I pull over at the next town to call her.

But first I discover a text message from Aiden. My gut clenches before I open it, but it's simply a request to let him know when I'm safe for the night. He's not making it easy for me to break the strings between us. I know his request is sincere and the part of me that dares to hope for a happy ending after all surges to the fore. I push it back relentlessly and call Ing.

"Rose? I was just thinking about you!"

"Would you be open to a house guest for a few days?"

"Seriously, you have to ask? Get your ass over here."

"Okay. I wanted to make sure before I bought a ticket."

"You okay, babe?" Her voice gets soft with the implied question.

"No. But I will be. Eventually." I attempt a smile, "On the bright side, the new book is done."

"Oooh, I can't wait to read it! Congrats, Rose."

"Thanks. I'd better get going, I just pulled off to call you so I should get back on the road. I'll let you know when I've got a flight."

"Sweet. Can't wait to see you, Rosey."

"Ditto." And we hang up.

Unfortunately, I hit San Diego right at rush hour so it takes a while to make my way to the outskirts of the airport. By the time I pull into the long-term lot that has space available, my right ankle is aching from having to hit the brakes so often.

I have to wait out in the blazing sun for the shuttle to take me to the airport. So when I'm finally standing in front of the most likely airline counter being told that it will be at least three days before I can get on a flight without paying through the nose for first class, I'm peeved. Okay, I'm fucking pissed off, but I try to rein it in and not be one of those customers.

I make my way down the line of counters and get the same story until one enterprising rep tells me if I'm willing to leave in an hour and spend the night in Cleveland, I can be in Raleigh by noon tomorrow. I take it.

27

Aiden

For about half an hour after she left, I try to pretend that Rose was never in the cabin. It didn't work. So I give up, pour myself a glass of wine, even though it's only two in the afternoon, and sack out on the couch with my phone to read Rose's manuscript.

For a brief second before I start reading I roll my eyes at the picture I must represent, a grown man, until recently a Naval officer, stretched out with wine and a steamy romance novel. Linda would laugh her head off. If I'm feeling really generous, I may tell her one day. We'll see after I read this masterpiece.

Of course, I lose track of time as I follow the romantic entanglements of Lena and Trevor, Rose's main characters. She did a good job. They're engaging, and it's not long before you're rooting for them to be together. The sex is... off the charts. There's an added layer of emotional anticipation that wasn't really there in her earlier books. Did I give her that? I certainly didn't manage to instill any knowledge of anatomy in her. The physics of what they get up to still require impossible feats of gymnastics. But just like her legions of loyal readers, I don't really care that much.

I keep reading. At this point, I'm following parallel tracks. There's the written story and the characters and then there's Rose, whose voice I hear reading the words. A slight stutter when she hits the dirty words because she is seriously sweet to the marrow of her bones.

At about the 60% mark, I feel a twist in my belly. At first, I think I'm getting hungry or need to eat something to soak up some of the wine. I get up and make a quick sandwich, continuing to read while I eat.

Then I finally realize what I'm feeling is pure and simple jealousy. This book is not about me. And it's pissing me off. Even though I know it's not about anyone else real. I'm well aware that Rose wrote the entire thing within the four walls of this cabin while I sat across the room most of the time. And most particularly because I *told* her to write it that way.

She still managed to write twenty-five pages of sex involving a cock that is definitely not mine. Exactly what I asked her to do. The next time someone looks around for an illustration to match up with 'dog in a manger' they're going to find a portrait of me.

I dial her number, determined to find out if she was watching porn on her computer when I thought she was writing. (Yes, I'm aware this is a stupid question to ask a woman, but in my defense, I'm too pissed off to think clearly right now.) Perhaps it's in my best interest that my call goes straight to voicemail. Only now I'm worried. Is she okay? Is she still driving or has she stopped for the night? She hasn't responded to my earlier text message.

I keep reading until I finish the book. Then I get up and find the bottle of Scotch I stashed in the back of the cupboard, intending it to be a surprise for Tris and throw back a shot. I'll buy him a new bottle or a fucking case of the stuff. The sunset, so similar to the one Rose made me watch, is lighting up the sky outside the picture window.

I check my phone, wondering where she is and if she's safe for the night. Will she even bother to respond to my message? Just as I'm staring at the display, a notification pings. Rose sent me a picture of a boring beige hotel room with only *I'm fine* underneath it.

I breathe out with relief. I know I can't expect her to check in with me daily. I don't have that right, but for now, she's safe and I can figure out where the hell I went wrong outside of touching her. Because damn my soul, I'm done having any regrets about that.

28

Rose

It's past noon when my flight lands in Raleigh. There was one of those mysterious parts problems that delayed the plane leaving from Cleveland. The early departure time I got up and checked out of my hotel at four A.M. for. I could have slept in. At least until a rational hour like seven. I could have had a real breakfast instead of trying to find the most palatable shelf-safe muffin in the tiny airport bookstore. Those ones that are oddly soft inside the crinkly cellophane package, and yet the expiration date is over two years out? What the fuck am I putting in my body?

Oh God, now I sound like Aiden. I haven't heard anything more from him since he asked me to check-in. Maybe he's already erased me from his memory. Out of sight, out of mind. I wish I could be that lucky. My entire body remembers his touch vividly, and it misses him badly. It's almost like he's a magnetic force, and I've moved too far outside of it for my own good.

Although if I'm completely honest, I was missing him before I left the cabin. I haven't even tried to have an orgasm without him. I'm not sure why, but I think I'm convinced it would be vastly inferior, and the immediate contrast would show me in painful detail exactly what I've lost.

I had to practically tie myself down not to creep down the ladder in the cabin and ask him for one last time. He'd have done that for me, I'm pretty sure. His parameter was always the time we were together at the cabin. I'm the one that drew the line across our relationship before that. It was the right thing to do. I think.

Fuck. I miss him. I wonder how many years are going to have to go by before he's willing to be in the same space with me again. Without surprising him, because I'm not quite that cruel. Either to him or to myself.

In any event, here I am in the heart of North Carolina renting a car because I didn't want Ing trying to come all the way into the city only to have to turn around again.

The drive out to the coast is beautiful, but I'm thankful the rental car has working air conditioning. I'm excited to see Ingrid again. It's only been a month since we last saw each other, but it feels like a decade has passed. I'm tired from all the crowds in airports. After three weeks alone in the woods with only one other person, the hundreds of people streaming to and fro are jarring to all my senses. I liked the quiet of the cabin, not having to worry about who was watching us or listening in.

I carefully follow all the directions Ing gave me and pull up behind the cutest lavender cottage I have ever seen in my life. There's a beautiful cottage garden with pink and white flowers blooming in the — front? The side of the cottage not facing the ocean — and it boasts white shutters and a deep white plank porch that goes all the way around.

Ing comes running out and practically hauls me off my feet. "Rosey! You made it!"

I laugh and hug her back, "I'm here. In one piece."

"The Commander?" she asks quietly.

I roll my eyes, "Prefers to live a life of lonely solitude or some such shit. But he, um…" I'm blushing hard.

"Oh!" She tugs me towards the cottage, "We need wine."

I pull free to grab my bags and we head inside, laughing and catching up. The middle-age nondescript man two doors down who's been staring at me doesn't escape my attention, but I don't mention him to Ing until we're well inside the little cottage. "So who's your weird neighbor? The yellow place?"

"Oh, that's Fred. He's one of Justin's flunkies."

"How do you know that?"

"I asked him."

I gape at Ing and she just shrugs, "He was watching and following me but not being extra creepy about it so I finally went up to him and asked him what his deal was. He gave me his credentials, and I confirmed them independently. Even went to the local cops, but since he's not stalking me or threatening me and he's licensed, there's not too much I can do. I could leave but then I'll just have new flunkies I have to research. So I figure the devil I know is better than the one I don't. Besides, I kind of have fun messing with Justin this way. I'm planning on inviting some of the surfer dudes I met at the beach over. For a sleepover." She winks dramatically.

"Ing! Seriously?"

"Well, sort of. I already explained it to them so they know it's not an actual orgy on offer."

"Have you talked to him?"

"Who, Justin? No. He sent me a letter via Fred."

"An actual old-fashioned letter? Typed or handwritten?"

"Typed. His handwriting is shit, and he knows it."

"What did he say?" And I thought my thing with Aiden was weird.

"That he was worried about me, wanted me back in New York where he could keep an eye on me, blah blah, that I couldn't draw on my trust fund otherwise."

"So he still doesn't know…?"

"That I have an income through you? I don't think so, although he must have someone figuring out how I paid for this place. I think he's trying to wait me out. Lure me back when I run out of funds, but he didn't come right out and say it."

"What about Margot? Is she still…"

"Don't know, don't care. At least I'm not there to have my nose rubbed in it." Oh, she cares all right, but I'm not the mean girl that's going to point out the obvious.

"Right. Well, what's good for dinner around here? Can I take you out?"

"Of course! There's a fabulous place three blocks down, we don't even have to drive."

"Perfect. Let me grab a shower and change and I'm all yours."

29

Aiden

I did the right thing. Our lives are simply too different in terms of trajectories for anything long term to have worked out. I have no doubt Rose will mentally pack up her days with me like one of her first novels and put it on the shelf. Some fond memories, maybe learned a few things along the way, but not a book you take down to reread. She'll be fine.

And I am fine. Before Darla-gate as I'm now calling it, I never worried about Rose or what she was up to. That was Tris's job. *Is* his job. Once there's a little more distance between us, in terms of time and space, I'm sure I'll be confident that if I haven't heard from her then she's just fine. I refocus my attention on the task at hand.

I really am fine. All except my thumb. For some reason, I seem to have forgotten how to hit a nail squarely. Five times the hammer has connected with my thumb instead of the intended target as I fix some of the rotted boards under one of the gutters. I need to get the repairs done that I mentally committed to because I'm due to leave here in just a few more days. I'll be driving straight up to Washington to start house hunting. My apartment is already packed and just waiting for a moving address. I plan to mail the keys to the cabin back to Tris. We agreed on that when I collected them.

I need to keep my focus on the future. It's what got me where I am today. Diligence and hard work focusing on the job and being prepared for all eventualities. So why do I still have this sense of unease? Like I've forgotten to do something important.

I climb down the ladder to go in for lunch. I'm smart enough not to continue making the same mistake, so maybe some protein will help my coordination. I'm not in the mood for much fuss and bother, so I settle for a basic sandwich — whole wheat bread with lean chicken breast and lots of vegetables. It's okay. Rose would insist it have mayo and cheese plus a plateful of potato chips.

Looking around the cabin, I'm becoming convinced that it's really the problem. I see Rose everywhere here, so that's simply reinforcing the gap, reminding me of her. That and the shower still smells like her shampoo. Not sure how that's possible, but there it is. Maybe I should leave early. That will give me a few extra days to find the perfect house up north. Something tucked away out of town with plenty of quiet. A new house that doesn't smell like Rose, a house where she's never been, will bring everything back to where it should be.

I can always hire a local contractor here to take care of the outside improvements. It's going to be months before Tris gets up here again, so he'll never know. Quite frankly, he probably wouldn't even notice if I told him. Like a lot of talented docs, he doesn't always pick up on other details of life that are right in front of him. Thank fuck, because otherwise, I'd be having to confess that I've messed around with his little girl. I'm not sure I'll be able to look him in the eye without spilling it as it is. But there's Rose to consider. I'll cut my heart out myself before I'll embarrass her deliberately.

So yeah, time to pack up. Separate out the perishable food. Take a garbage run down the mountain so I don't have to stop and do that on my way out. Once I'm in Washington, I'll be putting all my energy into the new job and getting settled. I'll be so busy there won't be a stray minute to think of Rose.

I go to bed early, intending to take care of the last-minute chores like stripping the bed and doing the laundry first thing in the morning, which will still give me enough time to get on the road before lunch. But I wake in the middle of the night, my chest heaving, sweat dripping down my back.

A dream, that's all it was, I tell myself, forcing my breathing to regulate. I dreamt that Rose was beside me, warm and willing, curled against my side. And then she was fading in front of my eyes, begging me with panicked eyes to do something. And I had no idea how to help. My subconscious apparently felt the need to be blunt, I guess. Because it's not hard to figure out where it was trying to go with that. But I'll counter with it's probably all being fueled by residual guilt.

Rose

I'm having such a blast catching up with Ingrid. It's a relief, if I'm honest, to fall back into our roles as college buddies, holding back on living life to the fullest until something would prove a convincing enough symbol that it was time to take more risks. Darla was a pretty big one, and it took us a while to recover from the initial rush.

But I swear Ing talks more about Justin now that she's technically free of him than she ever did when we were roomies. I don't think she knows him any better now, though. I bite my tongue for the seventh time as she explains why Fred, Justin's minion, has been replaced for a few days by Tom. Tom is younger and much better looking, so I'm wondering if he's been sent to lure Ing into some kind of romantic entanglement that will put her back in New York. Or that could just be my fertile imagination because Tom just walked out of their surveillance cottage and can't seem to keep his eyes off my legs, which I have propped up on the porch railing.

"Hey, Rose?" Ing calls my attention over to her. Oops, looks like this isn't the first time she called my name.

"What's up, Ing?"

"Let's have a party!"

"Um, okay. You mean the two of us?" I'm confused I thought we were partying — as much as two adult virgins are likely to live it up, anyway.

"No. I mean a real party. Lots of people. Spilling out on to the beach in the moonlight. That kind of party."

"Okaaay. I don't know anyone here, do you?"

"One or two people, those surfer dudes I mentioned earlier. But some of them know a lot more people. I think I can do this if you're here with me." Her eyes beg me to go along with this plan. I'm not sure if it's because I'm a year older or because I'm just not in a party frame of mind, but unease washes over me.

I keep wondering what Aiden is up to. Is he going to start dating once he gets to his new town? He's so oblivious to how attractive he is, he's likely to be swamped by women and not even noticing what's happening until he's in their clutches. Okay, that's a bit over the top, but I'm still worried. I stood up for myself though, finally. So I'll be okay. The last thing I want is to attach myself to a man who's too nice to tell me to grow up and move on.

So maybe a party is a good idea. Maybe if I kiss someone else, I won't taste Aiden on my lips anymore. Even though I write crazy passionate romance, I'm not really a believer in the one true soul mate theory. I have no trouble believing that there are legions of handsome, honorable men in the world who would make an excellent life partner. I just haven't met any of them.

And whose fault is that? My little internal voice asks, snidely. *All mine,* I acknowledge. Not being willing to look doesn't mean they're not standing right in front of you. And with that little pep talk, I pop inside to grab a notebook so Ing and I can plan the most epic party this part of the coast has ever seen.

30

———

Aiden

I don't know exactly when I finally acknowledged what Rose really means to me. I think it was just south of San Francisco, but it might have been earlier. I wish I could say I immediately saw the error of my ways and started course correction. But it was another two days of wallowing in my own mental self-flagellation and misery as I drove north before I gave in and sought help.

Maybe if I'd been in a better frame of mind, I'd have thought twice or twenty times before calling my sister Linda for advice, but hindsight is truly a bitch.

"A-ten? It's not my birthday or Christmas. Why are you calling?"

"And hello to you too, big sis."

She humphs, she really doesn't like being reminded that she's four years older than I am. I don't know why. She reveled in it when we were kids.

"I thought you might like to know that you're going to love Darla Simone's next book."

"What!!! You've read it? But it's not even scheduled for release for another four months."

"I received an advance copy."

"Does that mean you figured out who she is?"

"I did."

"And…?" her voice is slightly exasperated.

"And what?"

"Who is she? Was she an old lover?"

"No. But…"

"But…? I swear, Aiden, it's like pulling teeth talking to you."

"Yeah, well. This isn't easy for me."

"What, dear brother, spit it out or I will… I'm not sure what but you won't like it."

"I'm in love with her."

"How can you possibly know that? And why do you sound so pissed off about it?"

"I know it because I just spent the last three and half weeks with her and I'm pissed off about it because she's only twenty-three!" I shout into the phone. Which I have to take away from my ear and glare at because Linda bursts out laughing.

"Oh my. I was not expecting that. Can we go back to the beginning? You know I think that's your favorite line so yes, let's start there."

She's enjoying this entirely too much and I'm clenching my teeth. "No. We do not need to start at the beginning. I just need you to tell me how to convince her to give me another chance because I royally fucked it up."

"So she's not with you now?"

"No." God, I sound like I'm sulking.

"Who broke it off?"

"It was mutual. I can't give her kids or the future she

deserves, Linda, and she wasn't happy that I wasn't willing to talk about a life together."

"Men! How can you all be so stupid?" I hear a thwack and then Todd's voice, "Hey what did I do?"

"You're here and you're a man," Linda tells him pointedly.

"Are you beating on your husband, Linda? I think I'm supposed to report that kind of shit."

"Oh, fuck off. I only hit him in the back of the head with a newspaper. An unrolled one at that, so I think he's not psychologically or physically damaged. Not much gets through that thick skull of his that's for sure."

"Pretty sure my love life is not Todd's fault," I add mildly.

"He was here. He can take one for the team."

Well, Todd and Linda have been happily married for twenty years, so whatever works for them, "Back to my problem?"

"Right. Why can't you give her children? Do you have problems down there?" she whispers and I groan. Why the fuck did I call her again?

"No. I do not." Now I almost feel obliged to get Rose pregnant just to prove it to Linda.

"Do you even know if she wants children?"

"No." I'm back to sulking. And possibly imagining Rose round with my child. I'm not nearly as opposed to the idea as I thought I would be.

"Un-huh. So you just decided what life she ought to live, and that you weren't the guy to live it with her. And she didn't stick around for more of that?"

"Barn door, dead horse, sis. How do I fix it?"

"You figure out why you're getting in your own way and fix that first. Then you ask her what she wants without making any assumptions. After a really groveling apology that involves shoes, jewelry, or chocolate but better if it's all three."

"She's not really into shoes," I mumble.

"A-ten, not all women are like fucking Carlyn. Which I still think is a stupid name, by the way. Stop letting her control your life. Grow up."

Ouch.

"Now I have to go, baby bro. Good luck! Keep me posted. Love you."

And she hangs up before I can get another word in. Well, that doesn't matter too much, anyway. Somewhere in there was a useful nugget. She's right, I have to figure out what's bothering me about being permanent with Rose because it's not Rose herself. I grab a legal pad and a pen and sit back against the headboard in my bland hotel room to figure this out.

I've been alone for a long time. That's my first item of self-reflection. Even when I was married, we operated as two distinct units sharing the same orbit. I can't remember if I ever thought about having kids with Carlyn. I cringe at the thought now, that's for sure, but back when I didn't think she was a witch? Can't remember even discussing it. Surely it must have come up at some point...

I also never asked Rose what she wants out of life. At least I made sure she wanted intimacy, but life goals? I don't think we laid that out on the table. Probably because I assumed I knew. And maybe I do, or maybe I'm wrong as fuck. I should at least be humble enough to ask. Once. I don't see myself doing multiple check-ins like some new-age life coach.

And if I'm going to truly consider a long-term — dare I say permanent — relationship with Rose, then we need to spend more time talking than fucking. So maybe it's a good thing she's not in the same house or town. At least for a while. And that's making another big assumption that she's even willing to talk to me at this point. But a part of me is arrogant enough to say she's too soft-hearted to hold out for long.

I'm also going to have to tell Tris. Not the details, obviously. My hand automatically grips the back of my neck as I try to think how to tell him that will leave our friendship intact. I'm already resigned to being punched. I'd be more concerned about that, but Tris isn't what you'd call athletic. I'm not sure he's ever punched anyone in his life. Fuck. Nothing about this is easy. I could — should? — walk away. Rose would never know I was reconsidering, so she wouldn't be hurt by it.

But I can't bring myself to do that. I have to at least try. Sincerely this time.

I'll fuck it up if I call Rose before I've had some sleep. And if I'm going to get any of that, I need some release. All this thinking about her, imagining finding her in my bed every night, has my cock rising like that's an imminent reality.

To spare the hotel maid a nasty job, although I'm sure she's dealt with it many times, I head into the bathroom and turn the shower on full and hot. Immediately my mind transports me to the cabin shower with my fingers buried in Rose's virgin little pussy. A few strokes of my hand down my cock has precum beading on the head. I remember the sounds Rose made when she came; her head flung back, my name on her lips. And that's all it takes. My balls draw up tight and my cock is decorating the shower walls with long spurts of cum.

A few minutes later I'm back in bed, thinking through my recent decisions, and realize I need to make another list. How not to be a dirty old man because there's still something about being with Rose that feels forbidden.

31

Rose

Ingrid's party is probably pretty tame by most people's college standards, but it's wild compared to anything I've ever experienced. A few of the surfer dudes started an illegal bonfire on the beach and half the crowd is dancing around it while smoking shared joints. All those guys seem to have odd nicknames that I can't remember because they don't even use them but instead constantly call each other 'dude'. So I just started referring to them all as dude in my head, it's easier.

I haven't felt the need to talk to any of them. Some guy, I think his name was Steve, just pushed me against the kitchen wall and kissed me without any hint that I was interested. I wasn't. He was already drunk and sloppy. If anything, it did the exact opposite of getting Aiden out of my system. I don't want a drunk boy, or even a sober one. So now I've invited myself over to Fred and Tom's place, Fred is back in residence, and we're hanging out on the porch, not really talking. Every now and then Fred will ask about me or Ingrid, but I only give him answers that I feel are sanitized for future Justin consumption. For example, he asked me what I do for a living now that I've graduated. And my response was that I was working in communications. Close enough, right?

Fred's an okay guy. He's just doing his job, I guess. And I can't blame him for enjoying the fact that this time it took him to the beach in the Carolinas versus a run-down city block in New Jersey. I don't bother asking him anything about Justin. Mostly because I doubt he knows anything we don't know already and well, quite frankly I've got my own problems. Ingrid can ask him anytime, or maybe she already has, I don't know.

Thankfully, Ingrid is not one of the people dancing around the bonfire. I think she's somewhere in the kitchen trying to make perfect hors d'oeuvres because she had a very different kind of party in mind deep in her heart. Although this looks like a pretty typical surfer party from what I've seen. I sigh and look over at Fred, "Any suggestions for telling them all the party is over?"

He snorts a laugh, "Tell them your neighbor let you know he's called the cops. Bet you they've cleared out in under five. Just make sure that fire is totally out."

"Thanks." I'm saying it for both the tip and the willingness to share his porch. I head down the shallow steps that lead to the beach. I walk up to the first dude I find. He automatically puts his arm around my waist but retracts it as soon as I hit that magic word, 'police'. The message spreads like wildfire, and they do indeed clear out in record time. Someone was at least conscientious enough to pour a bucket of water on the fire before they booked it. I poke at the charred driftwood with another stick, making sure there's no glow of embers, and then head back into the house. Ing is standing there, still holding a pan of miniature crab puffs with a potholder, her mouth hanging open.

"What happened to everyone?" she asks, bewildered.

I shrug. I'm not going to throw Fred under the bus for this one. "Big wave coming in. Nobody wanted to miss it."

"Really? Nobody said anything to me."

"Maybe they thought it would be too much for a beginner?"

I'm totally making this all up. Because quite frankly if someone saw a single big wave they'd better head for high ground and only then once they know for sure it's not a tsunami think about surfing. But I don't say any of this to Ing. I grab one of her crab puffs and bite down. "Hey, Ing! These are really good!"

"Thanks." She smiles shyly. "I've been practicing in between doing art. It's another creative outlet, I think, helps get my juices flowing."

Oh fuck. I'm now thinking about other juices flowing and the fact that mine didn't, not for any one of the guys that were here tonight. Now I feel old. Not old enough for Aiden's self-righteous ass, but way too old for this kind of party. And clearly, I'm getting mean. Time for bed.

"Do you want me to help you clean up now or in the morning?"

Ing frowns down at her crab puffs. "Morning, I guess. I can't believe it's just over just like that."

"Did you have fun?" I'm curious if her idea of a good time has diverged from mine that quickly.

"Maybe? Mostly I was enjoying the thought of Justin's reaction." Ah. I guess not then.

"Babe. Stick those in the fridge and go to bed. And try to put that blowhard in your past. Someday soon you won't care what he thinks about what you do."

She nods but looks deflated and I feel a little flat myself. I look around for any perishables and help her stash them in the fridge. Then we both flip off the lights and head to bed.

32

Aiden

Destiny Bay is a small town. You might not know how small just driving through because it sprawls over the hills leading down to the harbor. But I knew it as soon as I checked into the quaint Victorian bed-and-breakfast. The motherly Mrs. Holst not only had my basic info already memorized, but was offering up her single niece to show me around town. That's when I bit the bullet and fully committed.

"Sorry, I'm proposing to my girlfriend this week. I wouldn't want to start the wrong kind of gossip around town. Or make your niece feel awkward." Mrs. Holst's friendly smile droops a little bit, but she perks up quickly. I think she realized she had the news first and could be the one controlling the flow of information. It's a *very* small town.

I will also be in her bad graces if it ever appears I didn't reveal all. And now I'm thinking I'd better find someplace more private to live before I ask Rose to come visit. First, I need to talk to her. Before I make a new messy pile of assumptions that I have to untangle.

I take my bags up to my room. It's a bit fussy for my taste. Lace and ruffles everywhere, but it's clean and otherwise comfortable, so I'm not going to complain. But I will be calling some real estate agents first thing in the morning.

The windows look out over the harbor and there are lots of little boats scooting along in all different directions. I pull the plushy armchair over so I can prop my feet on the sill while I call Rose. I have quite a bit of groveling to do so I might as well be comfortable.

And I've delayed long enough. I hit dial and listen to it ring. Finally, there's a sleepy, "Aiden? What's wrong?"

"Nothing on my end. Why do you sound so sleepy? Are you okay?"

She groans and there's a long pause, "I sound sleepy because it's ten P.M. here and I've never been a night owl."

"So you're on the east coast?"

"Hmm-hmm. Is that what you wanted to know?"

"Not exactly, no. I have several apologies to make, besides the one for waking you up. Do you want me to call back tomorrow when you're more awake?"

I can hear rustling as she moves to sit up, "You are such a tease. No, I want to at least get the gist of what you have to say. If I have questions, I'll ask you to repeat it all tomorrow. Now, I'm listening."

She sounds so adorable I wish she were where I could scoop her up and kiss her in-between words. "I don't have any right to ask at this point, but I want forever with you, Rosebud."

"Go on." She finally says softly after a long painful moment of silence.

"And I owe you several heart-felt apologies for assuming you don't know what you want, assuming I already knew what you really want, and that you aren't old enough to know what you need."

"Anything else?"

"I love you and I also owe you shoes, chocolate, and jewelry or whatever will demonstrate my deep regret for hurting you and not taking you seriously."

"I don't need the stuff, Aiden, but I need you to treat me as an adult. I am not a pet or a trophy just because I'm younger than you are."

"I know. Does that mean you'll at least consider coming back to me?"

"Aiden. I never really left. I'm not standing outside your door or anything, but it's only been a week. If you think I can fall out of love that quickly, you don't know me at all."

"So you love me?"

"Of course I do! Okay. That's fair. I guess I never really said it out loud but good grief, I would never let a man I didn't love fully and completely touch me the way you did."

I breathe out the breath I didn't realize I was holding.

"We have a lot of talking to do, Aiden, if there's to be something real and lasting between us."

"I know. I was hoping you would make me a list of everything you want out of life, a future together, anything you can dream of or know for sure you want. I don't want to limit it to just what you can think of at the moment. Will you do that for me?"

Her voice is calm and quiet when she answers, "I can make you a list, but, Aiden? You haven't mentioned timelines here at all. I don't really want a long-distance relationship if it's unnecessary. I'm still getting this feeling that you're not entirely comfortable with the reality of us together."

I close my eyes tightly, and I see Tris's face. I know what I need to do. "I mean now, Rosebud. Well, next week anyway. I'm in Destiny Bay at a B&B, but I have to go out of town tomorrow, probably overnight. After that I'm all yours, work schedule excepted." And assuming I'm not in the hospital as a patient.

"I have some requirements."

"Okay. What are they?"

"I want you to fuck me properly."

I choke, "Um, care to explain?"

"You held back those few weeks we had together because you didn't want to commit to the unforeseeable future. I need you to prove that you've moved past that."

"You're right. And making love to you isn't exactly a hardship. Next?"

"There's a codicil. You can't put that off too long. As in not at all, but I'm willing to be practical."

"Keep going."

"I need to know if you have any deal-breakers. Is there anything that would make you send me away again?" Her voice is hesitant and I wince at what I put her through, thinking I was doing it for her.

"No, Rose, there isn't. I could be sued if I walked away from this job, but there's nothing that would keep me away except for you saying you don't want me. Even then I would probably stalk you for a few years."

I can practically feel her smile through the phone.

"Last one, I want to see your list too. We need to do an even exchange. I know there's going to be compromise required, but I don't want you giving in to everything I want just because I want it."

"But what if that is what I want?"

"You're too bossy to keep it up for long. I'd rather not pretend."

"I love you, Rose."

"I love you too. Now tell me what airport so I can book my ticket."

Rose

Aiden loves me. Really loves me. I hug myself with relief that what I wouldn't let myself hope for is actually happening. There's a lethargy in my bones that I recognize as withheld tension letting go.

I should go back to bed and take care of travel arrangements tomorrow, but I'm too excited. And a little anxious that I need to make it all happen right now. So I get up as quietly as I can and pad into the kitchen where my laptop is sitting on the table. I groan with disappointment when the earliest flight I can reasonably afford is almost an entire week away, arriving in Vancouver, British Columbia on Friday at two P.M. Well, I've been patient this long I can wait a little longer and I don't want to pull Aiden away from his first week on the job.

Ingrid comes into the kitchen where I'm seated at the table with my laptop still open. "You look excited." She smiles sleepily, looking slightly puzzled.

"Aiden asked me to come back. Permanently."

"Oh!" She sits down, putting her elbows on the table. "What are you going to do?"

"Fly out Friday morning."

"Don't you dare get married without me there."

I grin with relief. I don't want to rub my romance in her face when hers looks so hopeless. Nevermind that neither of us managed to move on like we'd promised. "Okay."

33

Aiden

Some things can't be helped. And the fact that I'm squished into a middle seat of economy class on a flight back to San Diego is one of them. If this doesn't prove I'm ready to commit to Rose, then letting her father punch me in the face should do the trick. I'm not entirely sure he will, and I owe it to both of them to make sure he doesn't break his hand if he does.

By the time it's my turn to get up and sidle down the aisle of the plane, I haven't been able to feel my kneecaps for hours. And then the line to rent a car (without a reservation) goes on for what seems like miles. Of course, when it's my turn there's nothing left but an ancient, gigantic Lincoln. I take it. At least there's room for my knees.

I drive on autopilot to Tristan's house. The car does not. Its engine desperately needs a tune-up and let's face it, this thing is so old it should be shot and put out of its misery. Still, I'm grateful enough when I park it on the street in front of the house. I didn't tell Tris I was coming, so now I have to wait until he comes home, which should be in a few minutes.

Sure enough, his calm and conservative SUV comes down the street and pulls into the driveway. I don't think he even looked my way. So I get out of the car cautiously. I'm honestly not sure how to minimize the shock of what I'm about to tell him. I've resigned myself to losing his friendship, (hopefully it's only temporary) letting him *try* to kick the shit out of me, (unlikely) or simply face into his deep and abiding disappointment.

Tris spots me and looks surprised. He glances at the car and his jaw drops. "Aiden? What are you doing here? And why are you driving that… thing?"

I can't help the smile, Tris holds onto ancient and useless stuff and even he can see this piece of junk is past its use-by date. "It's all they had left at the rental place. I need to talk to you, Tris, and this one is big. I owe it to you to say it in person."

He looks thoroughly confused, but he shrugs, "Okaaay. Come on in. Would a beer help?"

"Won't hurt."

I follow him into the house where he drops his briefcase and grabs two beers out of the fridge. He leads the way out to the patio that I'm now seeing as a pivotal location in all of this.

"You don't own a gun, do you?" I ask. I'm only half-joking, it's probably wise to inquire.

"No. Should I?" He's looking more and more nervous. Tris has a very creative imagination, and I'm probably only making things worse.

"No. Now show me how you make a fist."

"Aiden. What the hell is this all about?"

"Just show me, please." He does, and I look at his hand. Ugh. Someone needs to drag him to the gym on a regular basis, I would do it if I lived close enough.

"Yeah, okay. Before you hit me, maybe keep in mind you're

more likely to hurt yourself." I nod towards his fist. He looks down at it and then at me, his eyebrows hitting his receding hairline.

"Will you spit it out, why would I want to hit you?"

"Because I'm in love with Rose and I'm going to marry her."

See, the problem with Tris is when he's confronted by something he doesn't understand or he's really furious (something I've only seen once or twice) he goes completely still with no facial expression at all. It's like he's a statue and you have to wait for some kind of reaction to know which way the wind is blowing.

"When did that happen?"

"Last month. She, um, wrote something that revealed she had a crush on me that I found out about. I made her come up to the cabin with me to sort it out. From there things um, developed. I swear to you, Tris, I tried to walk away but in the end, I couldn't do it."

He's frowning, "Did you seduce my daughter?"

"No. I don't think so. It was a mutual attraction."

He's not buying it, but I can't make him believe me. I take a bracing swallow of beer, "I'm not expecting you to like it, Tris. I sure as hell wouldn't if I were in your shoes, but I owed it to you to tell you directly."

"She told me she was going to the beach."

I sigh, "I made her say that. You'd have worried otherwise."

"You mean worried about exactly what happened and that I could have put a stop to?" Now he's getting sarcastic, which isn't nearly as bad as I expected, but not exactly good either.

"No. Because that was not at all my intention when I told her to meet me there. I promise, Tris, I never thought of Rose as anything but your daughter until about two months ago. I hurt her by pushing her away because of the age difference, but I'm done with that. All pain comes to me, not her. Agreed?"

"Hmmm. I need to talk to Rose. Stay here."

He disappears inside. I stretch my legs out and contemplate my sins, real and imagined. And I wait.

Rose

The beach is almost completely deserted, which seems strange despite the slightly wild weather, but I'm trying to keep myself out of Ing's hair since I'm staying a few extra days. I don't want to crimp her plans to get some serious design work done, and staying to gossip and giggle will do just that. So I'm out here stretching my legs, enjoying the way the wind whips my hair into a tangled mess, and thinking about Aiden. Mind you, I'm almost always thinking about him.

When my phone rings in my pocket, I almost don't hear it, but I grab it just in time and press the answer button.

"Hello?" I respond hesitantly — I didn't have time to check caller ID.

"Rosey? Where are you?" It's Dad. I guess I waited too long to check-in.

"At the beach. Staying with Ing."

"Not saying you're at the beach when you're really with Aiden at the cabin?" Uh-oh.

"Um, Dad?"

"What happened, Rose? The truth, please. Did he take advantage of you?"

"No! Good God, Dad, if anything it was the other way around. Why are you asking all of a sudden?"

"Because he's here claiming he's in love with you and you're planning to get married!"

"Oh!" We hadn't gotten to the wedding phase of negotiations. He'd implied it plenty of times. But there's no ring on it, is there? Nope. Then a horrible thought occurs to me. Aiden is there alone with Dad, a pissed off Dad, "You didn't hurt him, did you?" I've stopped walking, turning my back to the wind so I can hear better.

"Well, that answers one question, anyway." My dad says dryly, "Rose, you're way too young to get involved with a guy his age."

"That's what he said." I sigh, "Dad, I'm twenty-three, not eighteen. I've been in love with him for years. This isn't just going to go away."

"You have? How did I miss that? It's times like these I could murder your mother for not being here."

I grin, everything's going to be okay. "Dad, he made a cheese pizza without adding any vegetables to it."

"Seriously? That puts a whole new light on things." He's half-joking, but I know he gets my point.

"I love him, Dad."

He sighs, "Okay, it's not like I can stop you but if he hurts you, I will find a way to… I don't know what but something horrible."

"I don't want him to lose you, Dad. Or vice versa. You've been friends too long to throw that away."

"Yeah, well. This is going to take a bit of getting used to, sweetheart. I'm not sure how much time that requires."

"Will you at least go on that fishing trip with him? It will make me happy."

"Maybe. No promises." Ah well, I tried. I think Dad will come around in a few months. It's new to him, so I guess I can't be too impatient.

"Love you."

"Love you too, Rosey."

He hangs up, and I turn back towards the cottage. I want to call Aiden to find out what Dad won't tell me, but I'd be interrupting so I'll wait for a bit. He has work on Monday, so he must be going to take a late flight out tonight or early in the morning. I still send him a quick text message telling him not to do anything stupid if he's tired and that I love him. I don't have to wait long before I get the silliest selfie ever of Aiden and my dad drinking beer. They clearly have no idea what they're doing with the camera, but at least I can see that they're both okay, which I'm sure was the point. And it makes me laugh. Might just have to use it as my new screensaver.

I pick up a few pretty shells as mementos and take three deep breaths of the salty ocean air before heading inside.

34

Rose

My remaining few days in North Carolina fly by. Surprisingly, Aiden and I manage to hash a few things out via text message, even with his job and the time difference. And there might have been a few phone calls late at night where he whispered really dirty, explicit instructions and I followed them to the letter. Much to my satisfaction.

I am so putting some of that in the next book, although you'll never read his exact words. I had to triple promise that when I told him what I was thinking. Although I'm pretty sure his demands to read my manuscripts in the future are less about his privacy and quite a bit more to do with finding new opportunities to get me naked. I'm not complaining.

Before I know it, I'm getting up at the ass crack of dawn Friday morning so I can drive the rental back to Raleigh to catch my flight. Ing seems more settled, and I got her to promise she'd have some non-drinking friends over the next time she threw a party, just in case. She got up to make me a quick breakfast and hand me a giant travel mug of coffee before waving me off.

I manage to make the drive, return the car, and check-in with the airline in record time. Now I'm sitting at the gate flipping through my previous text messages with Aiden and grinning like a fool. And there aren't even any dirty pictures. Even if there is a big age gap Aiden and I are more alike than we're different — neither of us wants naked pictures floating around corporate servers so it wasn't even a question.

The flight itself is boring. I've traveled enough to now consider that a good thing. And it takes a really long time to cross North America. Yeah, I know it took a lot longer when it was wagons. Or even cars. But I'm still stiff and feeling grungy when I finally stand up to get my bag out of the overhead compartment. And isn't it weird to spend five hours in the air only to arrive two hours after you left? And apparently, Vancouver is seventy degrees and sunny today.

A text message pings as soon as I turn my phone back on saying Aiden is already waiting for me as close to the gate as he was allowed to get. Which sounds like it's somewhere around baggage claim, but I know to look for him when I see other waiting people. Funnily enough, it's the woman walking next to me that finds him first. I hear her say to her companion, "Who the fuck is that and who is he waiting for?" Of course, I look to see who she's talking about, and off to one side Aiden's there looking all stern and serious with his perfect military posture (and damn gorgeous, of course). I ignore the women and walk faster. As soon as he sees me, his face brightens, and he holds out his arms.

Yes, I fly into them. I defy any woman not to. And clearly, I need to get there first before any of the other passengers get ideas. His arms close around me while his chin drops on my head. I smoosh my face in his chest and breathe him in. He put on that aftershave that I still don't know the name of. I guess I don't need to, now that I get the real man and don't have to pretend.

"Do I get a kiss?" I ask cheekily, finally lifting my head.

"Hmmm. I was thinking I should hold those back in case I need them in negotiations." His eyes are laughing at me. I narrow mine in response.

"So we're going to fuck without kissing?" Oops, I might have said that a little too loudly. Aiden rubs a hand over his face to cover his grin, "Think we'd better get you out of here, Rosebud, before you start a riot or get me arrested."

He drops a quick kiss on my lips and then takes my carry-on from me. We troop to the baggage carousel along with the rest of the passengers. I'm not planning on leaving again, so I brought everything with me that I took east. All my other belongings, which are mostly clothes and books, are still in Kevin's trunk. And I'm not sure what to do about that, but I'll figure it out sometime this week.

With my luggage collected, we make our way to Aiden's truck in the parking garage. He slings the suitcases in the back and slips my carry-on behind the seats, then helps me up. It's weird being in his truck in a completely different state. Well, different country actually, at the moment.

"So is it a long drive from here?"

"Hmmm? Destiny Bay is about an hour, but we're staying in the city this weekend."

"We are?" Ooh, I'm excited. I've always wanted to see Canada and never had an opportunity to do so.

"Yes. But I believe you requested to be thoroughly fucked, so don't expect to see beyond the hotel room this trip."

"That can't take all weekend, can it?"

He slants a disbelieving look in my direction, "Rosebud. You've already accused me once of holding back. Now I have something to prove."

Oh. Oh, my. I gulp and acknowledge my panties are now

thoroughly wet. I shift awkwardly on the seat. Aiden must have noticed because he shoots me the most panty-melting grin I've ever seen on his face. And that's when I really register that the guilt is gone. He doesn't have that aura of sadness about him that he did before.

"You don't feel guilty anymore, do you?"

"No. Not anymore. Some of that was having it out with your dad, and some of it was just sorting through things in my head."

"And neither of you hit each other or anything else?"

He shakes his head, "I'd have let him, you know, but I was still worried he'd hurt himself."

Part of me wants to defend my dad because he would have defended me, but Aiden's right. And I don't want him getting hit.

Aiden navigates the downtown traffic with ease, finally pulling the big truck into the underground parking garage of a massive high-rise hotel.

He takes my luggage out of the back and we find the elevator that goes to the lobby, "Do you want to get dinner out or room service?" he asks evenly.

Hmmm. It's still mid-afternoon here, but past my dinner hour on the east coast. "If it doesn't throw off your seduction plans, I'd really love a shower and then dinner somewhere Canadian."

He coughs slightly, "Rosebud, I don't know how to tell you this but you're not exactly a hard sell."

I grin, "That's not true, you just had an advantage before. Kind of like a special coupon. I can rescind that if you like."

"Doesn't matter, I still plan to take my time. Now, what do you mean by Canadian, exactly?"

"I don't know. Something I wouldn't get easily on the other side of the border."

Aiden just shakes his head like he still can't follow the way my brain works. "I have no idea what that would be. We'll ask at the desk."

And to his credit, he does. The concierge must be used to these kinds of questions because he writes down three nearby restaurants on a slip of paper branded with the hotel's logo without blinking. I'm suspicious and planning to research them before we head out. I don't want to encounter a 'Canadian' steakhouse that could be found in Omaha.

35

Aiden

I've never looked forward to fucking a woman like I am right now. Not really. It was either convenient or not. Mutually agreeable, or it didn't happen. I've absolutely never planned out an evening like this one. Although, I've also never stopped to consider what defines Canadian food. And I've spent more than one weekend in Vancouver when I was stationed nearby in Washington years ago.

I have fun watching Rose demand every last ounce from the experience. I intentionally asked for a room on one of the upper floors when I made the reservation. I have plans that are best suited to not having to worry about closing the blinds.

But first I need to get her fed and relaxed. Rose gets more and more excited the higher the elevator rises. It stops for us on the twenty-fifth floor, and Rose practically skips down the hallway. "You sure you're not jailbait?" I ask her. She just grins in response, her blue eyes sparkling, "Live a little, McBride."

It takes two tries to get the door open with the keycard,

mostly because I can't quite take my eyes off of her, but I push it open so she can explore first.

"Oh, Aiden!"

I follow to see what exactly has her excited. Hard to tell, really. She's twirling in the middle of the room, taking it all in. I shake my head and settle her suitcases in the corner. At some point, I need to get my bag out of the truck, but it can wait until after dinner.

"You want to hit the shower now?" I prompt her. Not that I'm impatient or anything.

"No. I want to research our dinner options first so I know what to change into." She takes the slip of paper from my breast pocket, grabs her phone, and sits down on the bed.

"Absolutely not," she mutters then clicks some more, makes a scowly face, and keeps clicking then she tosses the paper into the small wastebasket by the bed. She's starting to look disappointed and my heart sinks. I want her to have nothing but happy memories of this weekend. Somehow it feels like these two days will define our future together. Maybe she feels the same because she peeks up at me, "How far is Thatcher Street?"

"A decent walk but doable if you don't wear heels."

"Okay, let's try this place then. It's not labeled Canadian, but it is all locally sourced and includes wild foraged food."

"That actually sounds interesting." I've always been curious about eating wild foods. Never really done anything about it, but I find the concept of eating off the land fascinating.

"Yeah?" Rose smiles with satisfaction.

"Really. Shower?"

"Okay. If I didn't know better, I'd think you were impatient or something." She gives a sassy grin and goes over to her suitcases. I assess the hotel room for my later plans while I wait. I think it will do nicely. There's just one giant bed with a suede upholstered headboard and about three times as many pillows as normal people need. And a small kitchenette sits in the corner with a counter at just the right height. There's the usual two or three armchairs and a dresser with the large TV. The rest of the room is dominated by the floor-to-ceiling glass wall that gives a panorama view of the city and ocean beyond. The water is sparkling in the sunlight and the harbor bustles with late Friday afternoon traffic.

Steam is rising from under the bathroom door and I'm having to hold myself back from joining her there. I want to. I've missed touching Rose, feeling her cum on my fingers or my tongue. And I'm eager to let my cock in on that action. Plus, I've simply missed her.

Then she emerges dressed in a pretty blue sundress and I'm glad I waited. She slips some white sandals on her feet and grabs a small purse, "Ready? I'm starving."

"Then let's get you fed." I can hold off satisfying my own hunger for a couple more hours.

Rose

Dinner was surprisingly fun. I mean, I expected to have a good time, but I think Aiden was really getting into the menu. It was super early by local time, so there was only one or two other couples in the restaurant. He ordered way more than either of us could eat because he just had to try some of the dishes. Some of it was a bit weird, but my favorite was venison with salmonberry sauce. Now I'm wondering if there are salmonberries in Destiny Bay. I'm not going to go shoot a deer, but I'll bet I can find venison at a specialty market. We talked about the food and my flight but stayed away from the big topics that we both know we need to cover. I'm thinking tomorrow is ideal for that, and even if Aiden doesn't, I'm going to make it happen.

Tonight is for reconnecting — in every way possible. We walk back to the hotel and I'm window-shopping as we go, my arm looped through Aiden's. I'm pointing out interesting things that catch my eye, but Aiden gets quieter and his gaze grows more intense the closer we get to the hotel. There's the dead silence of anticipation in the elevator that almost makes me want to run so he'll have to chase me. But knowing Aiden, he'd misunderstand that. So I walk demurely down the hallway to the room.

Inside, he takes my purse from me and sets it on the credenza, then he bends down and kisses me. Thoroughly. It's different than I remember. It's still Aiden, but more *intense*. Maybe I didn't fully realize how much he was holding back. I'm biting my lip when he puts both hands on my shoulders. He's frowning down at me, but there's the smallest quirk at the corner of his mouth.

"I believe one of your quite correct criticisms is that we need a more even exchange of power?"

I nod mutely, wondering where he's going with this.

"So this is how we're going to do this for tonight at least. I'm in charge of how we fuck and you're in charge of when. Agreed?"

My brow furrows, "You mean besides right now?"

"There's one basic rule here, Rosebud, I'm not willing to hurt you, not any more than necessary, and I'd rather avoid it altogether. So step one is I'm going to eat your pussy until you come at least once, preferably twice."

I shudder at that, my thighs clenching. Aiden can do really amazing things with his tongue.

"I'll be doing that while you brace yourself on the window over there," he nods towards the floor to ceiling glass, "and take in the view. Now when we do that, is entirely up to you. It starts when you're completely naked and in position. That could be in thirty seconds or five hours from now. You decide."

"Aren't you going to be naked?"

"Not yet." He smiles at me like he knows exactly what's happening between my thighs. I could cum right here and now, the way my imagination is running riot.

"Take your time." He steps back and strolls over to a comfortable-looking chair. Then he sits down and smirks. I'm frozen where he left me in the middle of the room. I mean, I seriously love this idea. I don't have to take charge, but I am in charge. I watch Aiden out of the corner of my eye. I'm a little miffed that he seems so calm. Then I see how his pants are tenting and I relax. We're on the same page then, he's letting me set the pace and trying not to crowd me. Not that he ever really did, but I think we need this to create more give and take.

Doesn't mean I can't have fun with it, though. I bend down to take my shoes off and make a production of lining them up just so in the closet. I hear a muffled cough which makes me smile, then I unzip my dress and let it slide slowly down my arms and off my body until it's a puddle at my feet. I step out of it and let him get a good view of my very cute white eyelet bra and panties. I thought I might as well milk the virgin thing for all it's worth. Hmm. His face is turning kind of red and his hands are gripping the chair arms rather firmly. I reach back and unfasten my bra as gracefully as I can manage, letting it drop on top of the dress. Then I peel the panties off, stepping out with pointed toes.

Walking over to the window, I peek over my shoulder, "Are you sure no one can see me?"

He has to clear his throat before he talks, "I'm sure. You know what to do."

With a little wiggle, I place my palms on the cool glass and lift my ass.

In less than a second Aiden is behind me, gently toeing my legs apart. Then he's down on his knees, his tongue starting in on the torture.

I can't see him at all, not even in the minimal reflection of the glass. I take in the view while my pussy is wracked with sensation. He licks, he sucks my clit. He thrusts his tongue into my channel in a preview of what he plans to do with his cock. In no time I feel my body tensing, fighting the oncoming train. Then it's upon me and I scream. Aiden chuckles then continues to lap at my pussy, bathing my swollen clit in soft touches until the spasms recede to small tremors. I really hope this glass is strong because it's totally holding me up right now.

Slowly Aiden pulls back and then stands. He pulls me into his arms, his hands palming my ass while he kisses me, his lips still wet with my juices. It's dirty and erotic and I love it.

"Such a good girl, Rose." He's teasing me, his hands sliding along my slit from behind. I shift restlessly. I'm ready for more.

"The next bit is one of two parts, so pay close attention. I'm going to get undressed and sit back down in that chair. When you're ready, I want you to come and sit on my lap facing me with your legs over mine. We're going to see how much of my cock you can take on your own this first time. I don't think it will be very much. Then I'll make you cum on my fingers while I stretch you out a little bit. After that, again when you're ready, I'll ask you to get up and lie down on the bed with your hands over your head and your legs spread."

He doesn't wait for my reply, just steps back and starts unbuttoning his shirt. My brain is mush. Happy, very satisfied mush. I lick my lips when he's shirtless. He has the perfect amount of chest hair that narrows to a fine arrow pointing at his very eager cock. Aiden smirks at me as he folds his pants and sits back down in the chair like it's the most natural thing in the world to wander around hotel rooms naked. He tents his fingers and simply watches me. I detour by the kitchen for a glass of water, which I drain quickly. Then I can't help myself and I scamper over to his chair. He gives me a supportive hand as I climb onto his lap, trying to arrange myself as he instructed.

"Put your hands on my shoulders," he instructs me softly. His shoulders are rock hard but warm to the touch. My hands itch to go exploring, but then he places one hand on my ass and guides his cock towards my pussy with the other. Instantly, I know this is right. This is the man who was always meant to be in my most intimate places. That doesn't mean it's going to be an easy fit.

"It's alright, Rosebud, just relax," he murmurs in my ear and I try. He's not pushing in, not really so it doesn't hurt, but he's also not really going anywhere. The broad tip of his cock is sort of resting against my pussy. It feels good, but I want him inside me. He lets go of my ass and slips his fingers under me to pull my folds wide. His cock slips in about an inch. I evaluate the new sensations. Fullness, stretching, belonging. But I know that's only the beginning. Like a foyer of a house, he's not *really* inside.

I wiggle and try to push down on him, but he's moved his hands to my hips and stops me. "Just feel me there, Rose. Introduce yourself to my cock." I try to relax and as his fingers trace small circles on my hips, I open enough to take another inch. I want to move, I need to feel him rub against my clit.

"So fucking tight, Rosebud. That's far enough in this position, for now, I think."

His touch changes to demanding as he reaches between us. He traces the seam where his cock meets my channel as if he's trying to slip a finger in there too, It's too much and my neck arches back with keening need at the additional pressure. My pussy floods with anticipation of a new visitor. Then he switches attention to my clit. It's different now somehow. Stretched from behind by his cock, it reacts more quickly to his touch, the scrape of a fingernail and I'm flying apart in his arms. My pussy spasms futilely against the short length of cock it's received, desperate for the rest of it. But Aiden is praising me, whispering words that promise me I'm all his forever.

I sink back down against his chest, panting. Wondering if I can really handle having all of him. It's like he can read my thoughts because he reassures me instantly, "It's going to get even better, Rose, I promise. Remember when you're ready, get up and go to the bed."

How am I ever supposed to move again? Aiden's fingers comb through my hair. If it wasn't for his still throbbing cock barely inside me, I'd think he wasn't in any kind of rush.

37

Aiden

In the beginning, I mistook Rose's lack of artifice as a sign of her youth. Now I know it's an essential part of her, and I'm the luckiest man on the planet to be on the receiving end of her unfiltered reactions. I'm also the most tortured because I've been hard for *hours*. But tonight isn't about me and my cock won't fall off or explode even if it feels like it.

Earlier in the week, we discussed via text message that we can skip the condom. The feel of her hot, wet pussy against my cock adds to the almost irresistible urge to thrust as hard and fast as I can. Not tonight.

Slowly Rose peels off my chest, looking flushed and dazed, her eyes unfocused. I let her take her time — that is what I promised her, after all. Once she lies down on the bed, I'll seize control again, but not until then. Even if it kills me. She blinks a few times and then smiles. "I'm ready now, I think."

I nod. "You know what to do." I extend my hand to support her as she stands. Her thighs glisten with evidence of her arousal, her breasts turgid. The path she takes to the bed isn't straight. It's the meandering curve of someone tipsy, but I know she hasn't had any alcohol. She stretches out on the sheets with a long relaxed sigh and for a brief second, I'm afraid she's going to fall asleep. Her mouth curves seductively as she raises her hands to the pillow behind her. Her back arches with the change in posture and those perfect breasts are now proudly displayed. Her graceful legs splay open, the rosy-red folds of her pussy proving her body is ready for me.

There's a part of me that still can't believe she's mine. But it probably never will, so I'm learning to ignore it. I give her a few more seconds of anticipation and then I'm kneeling between her thighs. I can't resist giving a little attention to her breasts, they've been begging for a while now, and lastly one deep kiss, "You ready, Rose?"

She nods and as slowly as I can manage; I hold her hips and push into her achingly tight pussy. She's relaxed, that's why we did a little exploratory practice and I keep up the steady pressure. If her barrier is still intact, there's not much there, thank God, and it's more about letting her adjust to my size.

"So full," she sighs, sounding delighted.

"You like that, Rosebud? Being stuffed full of cock?"

"Um-hmmm, yours anyway. Don't really want to try any others."

"Better not," I growl my pace increasing unconsciously with the need to claim her as mine. When I'm fully seated, I pause, letting her take her time until she starts to wiggle, shifting slightly from side to side.

"Need you to move, Aiden."

"You sure? Does this hurt?" I pull out slightly and slide back in. She's tight but fitting against my cock perfectly.

"No, feels good. Just need more. I need to cum."

"At your service, Rose." And I mean it. She may accuse me later of holding back but that's only because I don't want to break her in two so I keep everything at about fifty percent of what it would be if I was out of control. Her hands are shifting, moving down, trying to reach for me. I know she's close and my balls are so tight up against my body it's like they're trying to go back inside. I won't last long either. I pull almost all the way out and give her several fast shallow thrusts, teasing her g-spot, pulling back out before she finds that friction she needs. It ramps up her release quickly and when I push back into her fully, her orgasm explodes around us. Her back arching off the bed, her pussy spasms tight against my cock as if only just realizing there's something there to squeeze. She milks my cock for all it's worth, and my cum shoots into her womb with a force that makes me fall forward over her. Her arms instantly wrap around my back, binding us together.

As soon as I can form words, I make sure she can breathe and ask, "You okay, Rosebud?"

She gives me a happy sigh in response. Words come a few minutes later, "That was worth waiting for."

"I'm glad."

She swats ineffectively at my arm, "Is that the best you've got? You're glad?"

"I'm over the moon with delight that you're going to let me fuck you like that for the next forty years at least. Better?"

"Damn straight," she says with a grin.

She protests again when I pull out, which is a double shot to my heart and my ego. "In a few days, babe, we can stay there longer. Now I need to clean you up and let you recover."

Her pout is broken by a small yawn so I fetch a warm washcloth and minutes later tuck her up against my side as she falls asleep.

38

Rose

As I wake up, I stretch without opening my eyes. Abdominal muscles I didn't know I had twinge when I move on the cool sheets. My eyes pop open at the unexpected soreness to assess the situation. My gaze lands on the wall of windows, where my handprints are clearly visible. Oh yeah, last night. I grin with satisfaction and that's when I see Aiden already dressed, sitting in one of the armchairs with his legs stretched out so his feet are resting on the bed.

"Hey," I say softly. He looks so stern I'm not sure what's going through his head.

His face immediately softens, "Morning, Rosebud. How do you feel?"

I stretch again, "A little sore, not too bad. Hungry. Happy. What are we doing for breakfast?"

"Room service. I wanted you to sleep as long as you needed."

"Why were you looking so serious?" I pull the covers back

so I can go brush my teeth. I take a certain amount of satisfaction in watching his gaze heat as I stand up.

"I was thinking that I don't deserve you, but I'm keeping you, anyway. And wondering how many times I can fuck you today without being a dirty old man."

"How about as many times as I want?" I drop a kiss on his forehead as I walk by. He tries to grab me but I swivel away with a giggle, "Morning breath!"

I brush my teeth and put on one of the hotel bathrobes. When I come back out of the bathroom, Aiden hands me a mug of coffee and I toss pillows back on the bed before settling in against the headboard.

"What do you want for breakfast?"

"Hmmm, Bacon and scrambled eggs with hash browns, I think."

Aiden frowns at me, and I roll my eyes. We haven't gone over our lists yet, but this is one of my items, "You're free to get oatmeal, you know."

He lets it go and calls down with our order.

"So when are we going over our lists?" I ask, twirling the end of the bathrobe belt between my fingers.

"After breakfast, after I make love to you again?"

I smile, "I like that agenda." I look over to the window, "Um, can you wipe that glass before they get here with food?"

He looks puzzled and then smirks, "No. I want you right back in the same spot later."

"Oh." I gulp. I'm not sure I can take a full repeat of last night. But maybe he has something else in mind?

Maybe I'm a bad influence, but when our food arrives (which Aiden intercepts at the door) his plate has a gorgeous omelet on it. Not a grain of oatmeal in sight. It buoys me up. Not that there's anything wrong with oatmeal or eating healthy unless it sucks the joy out of the room, that is. The food smells amazing. Does having really bountiful sex improve your senses? In any event, I practically inhale the bacon and make short work of the rest of it.

Aiden stands and takes my plate with a quick kiss on the lips, "Same as last night, Rosebud. Whenever you're ready, naked in position at the window. I'll take it from there."

I need another cup of coffee first. I watch him over the rim. There is zero sign that he's aroused or impatient or doing anything other than reading the financial section of the newspaper the hotel left at the door. Except that he hasn't turned a page in five minutes.

Now I'm the one smirking as I rise from the bed, loosen the robe, and let it fall away as I saunter over to the window. I don't look back.

And I don't have to wait too long until large hands are reaching around me to cup my breasts, taking their weight and rubbing my nipples into painfully stiff peaks. Then he abandons them, one hand sweeping my hair off my shoulders as he nips and sucks along the line of my neck.

He doesn't speak, just telling me what he wants with his hands that move and guide me into position. A thick finger tests my readiness and then swirls around my clit a few times. His hands grip my hips and then I feel his cock nudging my entrance. I want it; I want to take my hands and push it in me now. But I'm braced at such an angle that I can't, not without falling forward, so I have to wait. Wait as Aiden enters me one millimeter at a time with a muttered, "Fuck, you're tighter than you were last night."

"Just take me, Aiden. I won't break."

"Not going to hurt you, either." He responds and pushes in a little further. Something shifts, maybe it was his hand playing with my clit, maybe it was the surge of wetness I felt leave my body but he slides home and I yelp a little at the suddenness of being full, feeling all of him *right there.*

He gives me a few seconds to acclimate and then he's

pounding into me, building into a punishing rhythm that has my forehead resting on the glass, my mouth slack. He pinches my swollen clit lightly and I moan as all the building sensations cascade over me in a mighty burst. My pussy clenches hard on his cock, stopping it in its tracks like a vise. He pulls out and pushes in, groaning as my body clamps down, trying to milk him dry. He shudders against my back as he cums. I spasm around him a few more times and then we're both spent. I'm not convinced either of us will be able to move ever again.

Eventually, though Aiden carries me into the shower where he washes me tenderly and dries me off.

The rest of Saturday passes in a rotation of napping, fucking, and eating. I made Aiden go down and get food somewhere else because I thought the number of trips from room service was getting embarrassing. He raised his eyebrows at that, but did it, anyway. On his return, he demanded a tip though, and that's how I found myself sitting on the counter of the kitchenette with his face between my thighs. Not that I'm complaining.

39

Rose

I feel like we're going into business negotiations as I get dressed. Aiden pours me a fresh mug of coffee and I sit down demurely in a chair. We exchange pieces of paper. I have a pen and notepad. He has a clipboard. (Who the heck brings a clipboard to their hot weekend away with the girlfriend? Aiden, apparently.) Except he spoils the whole business-casual thing by bringing my feet up to his lap and proceeding to massage my toes. "Stop trying to seduce the opposition." I try to frown at him, but honestly, that feels so good all I can manage is a sappy smile.

"Rosebud, we're on the same side. That's the point. Now read over my list while I study yours."

Now I really am frowning. I want to watch his face so I can guess what items he might balk on. But I have to trust him when he says he plans to work it out, otherwise, what am I doing here?

I unfold his piece of paper. And promptly roll my eyes at the first few items:

1. Make Rose feel loved

2. Fuck Rose on a very regular basis, preferably daily

3. Wake up to Rose (then fuck her)

4. Watch the sunset with Rose

Then I just have to smile:

5. Find a house that Rose loves

6. Buy Rose a safe car

7. Convince Rose to go back to using me as her hero

8. Marry Rose asap

9. No kids the first year, then a firm probably if Rose wants them

He went a lot easier on me than I did on him, but then I think we both expected that. I look up to watch him read. He's taking notes. He frowns, looks over at me, then jots something down. He reaches down and caresses my ankle with his free hand.

"I have some questions." He finally swings his gaze fully to me.

"Okay." I shrug, I expected some.

"What do you mean by number three, Don't tell me what to eat?"

"I mean that I am not a child and you are not my parent. Or even my doctor. If you're cooking, I don't expect you to make anything special for me. I'm not allergic to anything as far as I know, but if I'm cooking or we go out or we're at the grocery store, my choices don't need to be your choices. If I want to make brownies and eat brownies, I don't want to hear about what that will do to my waistline or my arteries."

Aiden rubs the back of his neck as if he's struggling with this concept. "I understand what you're saying, but I can't promise that won't take some practice. Or that I won't try to do most of the cooking."

I grin at that. And it's not like Aiden doesn't hover over Dad's eating too, so it's not just because I'm so much younger. "That's fine. I'm happy to remind you."

"And what is a non-ostentatious engagement ring or other jewelry? I know what the words mean, but that seems pretty subjective."

"Then I will be happy to point things out when needed, but nothing to impress the hospital wives' club. I'm not into that shit."

"Good God, that's a thing?" He looks astounded.

"Of course it's a thing!"

"Hmmm. Just a second." He moves my feet over and stands up. Over where we dropped our luggage he rummages through his bag and then walks back towards me, "How's this on the ostentatious scale?" And he holds a vintage Art Deco diamond ring out to me, but won't let me take it from his fingers.

"It's perfect." I sigh with longing. It's probably the most beautiful ring I've ever seen. Aiden kneels beside my chair, taking my left hand. "Then, Rose Serena McClelland, recent virgin, will you marry me?"

I wrinkle my nose at that title but give in, "If you drop the former virgin part, then yes, I will."

He slips the ring on my finger, drops a kiss on my palm, and goes back to his clipboard, enthusiastically making a mark, "Good, that's one thing checked off."

I burst out laughing. "What else?"

"Umm, I think that's it. The house stuff is all good, you can work with the real estate agent on those. Are you sure about the kids?"

"Yes." I shrug. "I think I might want them someday, but definitely not for a year or two, and then we can talk about it. I don't need to be pregnant to feel satisfied with my life, Aiden."

"Okay. Just talk to me if that changes."

"Promise. And I think we should do this every year, anyway. Hopefully, in this same hotel room."

His lips twitch a little at that. "Fond memories already, huh?"

"I think so. Now one last thing. We need to talk about your request to be in all my books. That's a bit of a turnaround so...?"

Aiden shifts uncomfortably looking down at his hands, "I realized when I read your manuscript, that I was jealous. Even knowing you didn't base it on a real person." There's a hint of doubt in his voice that makes me think he's not a hundred percent confident of that. I wait him out. "And even though I don't want anyone else to know, particularly Linda, *I'd* like to know that I'm still your ideal romantic hero."

I bite my lower lip because — because he couldn't have said anything more perfect. I pull my feet out of his lap, jump up and throw myself at him. He looks a little surprised but pleased to find me in his lap. "How about this, I'll make sure you know when you read the book, and you'll always be the first to do that, that I was thinking about you and your cock every single time? And you can give me suggestions for the details that will throw everyone else off. Like... I dunno birthmarks or a tattoo on his butt or something."

"Do I get my name on the cover too?" Now he's just teasing me.

"If you're not careful. I'll make sure each and every one is dedicated to the man that inspired it all." I half expect him to gag at that level of sweet drivel, but he's eating it up with a spoon. Aiden definitely needs more sweetness and light in his life, and I'm going to see that he gets it. Only fair, I suspect I'll be eating a lot more quinoa and hummus than I would ever consume on my own.

This time when I wake up, I'm nestled on top of Aiden. The rise and fall of his chest is gently soothing. All I want to do is curl into him and stay like this forever. He must sense I'm awake because his hand starts to slowly massage my spine, moving from my tailbone up. "Mphh," I sigh with pleasure, my voice muffled against his skin.

"Morning, Rosebud."

I answer with my fingers, rubbing them gently against his flat male nipples. Talking is overrated.

Aiden captures my fingers with his hand. "I'm sorry I hurt you at the cabin, Rosey. I should have realized sooner I could never walk away from you."

I support my chin on my hands, my arms folded on his chest so I meet his solemn blue eyes. "Have you been awake worrying about that? Don't you think it was inevitable in a way? I mean, we had to come together to know there was... something there at all."

His face doesn't relax from its stern lines so I sigh and try again, "Tell me the truth, if you and I had crossed paths for the first time in a bar, if you'd seen me across the room, would you have come over to talk to me?"

His answer is swift and abrupt. "No fucking way."

I pout because jeez.

"I'd have looked for sure, possibly watched you for a while, maybe even jerked off in the shower later thinking about you, but I wouldn't have approached."

I nod, it's what I expected even if it hurts a little, "So it shows great foresight on my part to have been born into the family where you couldn't avoid me."

That makes Aiden grin, "You trying to say I was set up?"

I nod solemnly but can't hold back the inevitable giggle. "You see where I'm going though. We had to have a transitional meeting, the thing that made space to see if there was anything to pursue. Making a long-term relationship happen is a different project phase, requiring a different set of decisions. So I don't think there's really anything to have deep regret over... except for one thing."

"What's that?" His voice is low and solemn, slightly curious.

"You're whole not going to fuck the virgin hangup. That was completely unnecessary and I expect retroactive compensation. With interest." I try for a stern face with a hard glare.

I have no idea if I succeed because suddenly I'm under Aiden, his cock pushing insistently at my pussy while rubbing against my clit. A growly voice mutters in my ear, "What sort of interest rate are we talking here?"

"Criminally high," I stutter as he surges into me.

Aiden makes a serious dent in his debt before we eventually get out of bed. We're leaving Vancouver this morning. It's time to go see my new hometown and I'm kind of excited.

Since we need to check out in a few hours, this morning I get breakfast in a restaurant. Not that I'm really complaining about room service followed by window fucking, but it's really fun to try local places. If Aiden had his way, I think we'd just take the elevator to the hotel coffee shop, but I won't even entertain that option. Instead, I drag him outside and down a few side streets until I find this quaint little cafe that promises real British crumpets along with the usual breakfast stuff. And the thing is, Aiden has fun too. He just never expects to, so it sneaks up on him. Kind of like me.

What Aiden assures me is supposed to be about an hour trip (although he doesn't have too much firsthand knowledge either) takes more than twice that because there's some kind of backup at the border crossing. We're in line to re-enter the United States, inching forward with long pauses, and I decide now is the perfect time to do a little window shopping on my phone. Why not scroll through gorgeous beds when he's right next to me and I can get his opinion?

Except all he's offering is a few non-committal grunts when I show him some of the ones I really like. I do my best facial impression of a doe-eyed innocent, widening my eyes and blinking, "All I want, Commander McBride, is to be guided by your superior age and wisdom." Blink, blink.

A glare that could fry an egg comes at me sideways, but his lips twitch, "Watch it, Rosebud, or I'll guide you right onto my cock." He lowers his window for the customs agent right as he says the last word, leaving me blushing and squirming while wondering how much the guy heard. Of course, he doesn't say anything and I bite my lip until we're through the gate so I won't either.

Aiden reaches for my hand when he's done merging back with the other traffic. He kisses the palm, folding my fingers over it, and then gives my wrist a small love bite. "As long as it's a California King and has a decent mattress, I don't care. Find the bed you want to be fucked on the most. I'll give you the budget numbers when we get to the B&B and you can figure out what goes to the house and what you spend furnishing it."

"Are you going to be pissed if I put some of my money in there too?"

"Rose…"

"I'm only saying I've been saving to get a place of my own, anyway. I already paid off Dad's mortgage, so why wouldn't I contribute if it means getting exactly what we want?"

"You paid off your dad's mortgage?" He sounds astounded.

"Yeah, I didn't want him worrying about it. Mom's medical bills were high and then my first two years of college, and well you know Dad, he's better at giving than receiving."

"Yeah, he's a good guy. That was a really generous thing to do, Rose."

I shrug. I didn't do it for the applause. And it's not like I have any other family to spoil. "So you're okay with it?"

Aiden rubs the back of his neck, which means he's really not but doesn't want to say it. I roll my eyes to myself and think about what I could get him for his birthday that would cost as much as what I'm prepared to put into a house.

"How about we look at what the total budget would be if you put in fifty percent of what you have saved? If we need it for the house, fine, but otherwise I buy the house and you buy all your fancy furniture."

I lean over and kiss his cheek, "Compromise looks good on you, Commander."

EPILOGUE 1

Rose

6 Months Later

I find it fascinating to see the different perspectives of a person. I've known Aiden as my dad's best friend my whole life, my crush for years, and my lover for not very long at all. But now I get to see him as someone's little brother, and I can't stop grinning with delight.

Linda is hilarious. She arrived like a hurricane — there was a little bit of warning, but neither of us was truly prepared. She's a shorter, rounder version of Aiden and she doesn't listen to him at all. She swept into the living room, gathered me up in a full-body hug and dropped me down in another room entirely saying, "Oh! I'm so excited to meet Darla! Are you sure I can't tell people I know you? I have to confess I told Aiden to sue you, but that's when I thought you were some scorned lover taking advantage of him. I'm going to make it up to you by spilling all his secrets. He's so annoying, isn't he?"

She pauses for breath and I blink. I'm not going to take sides against him, even if I will admit that he can be a bit bossy.

Her eyes glint with evil delight, "Did you know that when he was little I used to make him wear dresses and pretend he was my little sister?"

I look through the archway at Aiden, the epitome of elegant masculinity, where he leans against the kitchen counter talking with Linda's husband, Todd. My expression must have telegraphed my astonishment because he calls to me, "Whatever she's telling you is completely unfounded."

"Oh, it is not!" Linda exclaims. "He's just lucky he predates social media. *Somebody* destroyed all the photographic evidence."

"There were pictures?" I'm breathless, trying not to laugh.

"Oh yes, our mother thought it was hilarious. I might be able to put my hands on one or two still if I ask the cousins. There was a particularly good one where I made him wear a sunbonnet in addition to the dress."

"Oh, my." The giggles burst the dam and I'm having to wrap my arms around my stomach to keep my ribs from hurting. Linda sits back, looking pleased with herself. There's a twinkle in her eye that tells me she adores her brother but will never, ever admit it.

Aiden saunters in. Without warning, he scoops me up and sits down with me on his lap. I push at him ineffectively. I don't think we need to make out in front of his sister. Apparently, he has other ideas. He pinches my waist lightly in warning and then proceeds to tease me until I'm fidgeting and probably turning red in the face. He keeps everything out of sight, tracing naughty words on the center of my back and otherwise trying to distract me. When I feel my pussy flood after he spelled out *swallow my cum,* I finally say with exasperation,

"Aiden!" He gives me a wide-eyed innocent look that's entirely overkill while Linda laughs, "Told you he's annoying. Anytime you need to escape come visit me and we'll commiserate."

I blush, and Aiden turns my chin towards him with a firm hand. He kisses me, his eyes locked on mine, pulling back just enough to grumble, "Go away, Linda."

She doesn't of course. We're getting married this weekend. It would have happened sooner but getting Dad and Ingrid here took some planning and then there was the whole debate about whether Dad should walk me down the aisle or be Aiden's best man. I didn't care and told him to choose whichever would give him the best memories, which didn't help at all. He finally decided to do both. He's going to walk me down the aisle and then stand next to Aiden. Plus, it took about three months for Dad to even get comfortable with the sudden change in Aiden's status to son-in-law, although we all agreed never to use that term. And Ingrid is arriving later today to be my maid of honor.

The house we settled on is my dream house, so I'm excited to show it off to everyone. And I've finally got things painted and furnished, mostly the way I want them. I didn't tell Aiden how much I spent on that, and he didn't ask. The house is older but with recent renovations, which means the kitchen meets Aiden's exacting standards and I have a non-drafty house to write in. It gets blustery up here on the bluff! We have a gorgeous view of the inlet and occasionally I get to see killer whales and even once a gray whale. I have to force myself to write in the back room sometimes if I find myself getting too distracted by all the wildlife.

It took a lot of looking to find just the right thing that was still a reasonable commute to the hospital for Aiden. He told me not to let that be an influence, but one item on my list was to have him home for dinner every night, so it didn't seem fair to make that difficult.

We're going back to Vancouver for our first honeymoon. It's just a long weekend this time, and then in the summer, we're going to take two weeks to go somewhere exotic. I keep bouncing between New Zealand (since I never did get there) and France (because I'm still trying to win Aiden over to the worship of all things cheese).

Oh, and the book I wrote in the cabin? It's still selling like hotcakes. But readers keep sending me emails that they like the other heroes I write better. All the ones based on Aiden. I read those aloud to him when I get them. To which he always smiles and replies something along the lines of 'don't mess with perfection.' I couldn't agree more!

EPILOGUE 2

Rose

Two years later

They say that the key to a solid relationship is communication, right? I'm not sure 'they' were talking about the kind of conversation I'm about to have with Aiden, but maybe they were. I'm a bit nervous as to how this is going to turn out, but nothing ventured, nothing gained. The sheer volume of cliches spewing from my mouth right now should give some indication of my anticipation.

Aiden's working from home today. It's Tuesday, which is his paperwork day. He has a love-hate relationship with the second day of the week because of it. I think he likes being home with me more than he's willing to admit, but he's never been good with the after details of closing files and final reports. I already checked his calendar, and he doesn't have any meetings. And if I don't do this today, there's a good chance he'll make me wait nine months before I get another opportunity.

He's taken over the small home office at the back of the house. It's dark and cold, but he says it suits his mood when he has to do work at home. Unlike my office, which is the smaller of the two guestrooms upstairs with sunlight pouring in and plenty of houseplants to liven up the rainy days. Enough digressing. I'm knocking on the door now.

"Rosey? Would you stop knocking on the doors in your own house?" He sounds amused. That's a positive start.

I stick my head in, "I'm just making sure you're not on the phone and give you a chance to hide your porn stash."

He rolls his eyes, "Someday you'll have to show me where you keep it." There is no porn stash, unless you count my manuscripts, which are in the closet in my office. I walk over to stand next to his desk. "Seriously, Aiden, are you in the middle of anything?"

"No, actually I'm done. I was just about to come find you, see if you want to go out for dinner later."

"Hmmm, not a bad idea. But first I have some research I need help with." I wiggle my eyebrows suggestively.

His eyes widen and he pulls me between his legs and leans in for a quick kiss, "I thought you didn't worry about accuracy in that department?"

"I don't," I confirm with a giggle. "It's all about mood, not physics."

"Then what can I help you with?"

"I want you to spank me."

He coughs violently, his hands gripping my hips tighten in response. "Come again?"

I knew this was going to be a hard sell. "I've been reading some new authors and then I was talking to Linda last week..."

"Stop right there, I do not want to know that my big sister thinks I should spank you."

"Relax, we didn't talk about you. She just wanted a little more variety in the next book and she's not wrong."

"And? You jump from there to reddening your ass?" Aiden's looking at me like I've lost my marbles and am trying to find them in the dark with my tongue.

I sit down on his thigh. This is going to take a while. "No. As I said I've been doing some reading, and quite a few authors who don't do the whole domination bondage thing *do* venture into a little light spanking. There's something about nerve endings and well where my clit would end up on your thigh..." He looks ready to say something so I hurry on with my leading argument, "Anyway, I don't want to open up that territory without making sure I'm okay with it. I'm a little on the fence. Is it only fun for someone that likes to be dominated or is there something more universal there?"

"I won't hurt you, Rosebud."

God, he's such a sweetheart behind the stern facade. I kiss him deeply to show my appreciation. "And you won't. I swear if it's not something we both enjoy, I'll never bring it up again. And I'm not asking you to go all out. No more than ten spanks, that should be enough of a test."

"Ten! I was thinking more like two." He's grumbling now, which means I've got him mostly there.

I take one of his hands in mine and drag it under the skirt of my sundress. "See? I already dressed for the occasion." By which I mean I'm not wearing any panties. His big hand starts to do a little exploring, sliding between my ass cheeks.

"Okay, just this once, but you tell me to stop and I'm done. How do you want this?"

I walk him through it one more time, bending myself over his thigh and lifting my skirt. I can feel his gaze on me. My pussy is already wet in anticipation.

What follows is anticlimactic at best. I can barely feel his hand on my butt. And I would definitely classify it as a caress, not a spank.

I sigh and put my hands on his thigh to push myself back up. "Okay, that's not quite what I had in mind."

"Hurting you is never going to be fun, Rose."

"It's just the good kind of hurt, babe. Like when I bite your earlobe. Like this." I demonstrate and instantly feel his cock respond against my leg. He *really* likes when I do that. "I have an idea. If this doesn't put you in the mood, then I'll go change and we can go to dinner and forget all about it. Deal?"

He eyes me warily, "What's the idea?"

"So little trust." I tease him with a smile. Looping my arms around his neck, I lean in and whisper in his ear, "So I have this idea for a new book. Yesterday I went into town (*I stayed home all day yesterday and he knows it*) and there was a bunch of hot young Marines (*he hates the Marines*) doing this toy drive (*it's also way too early for Christmas toy drives*) and it got me thinking. Do you think they can finger fuck a girl with those gloves on? It made me all kinds of wet just thinking about it. And they were so well coordinated. Be a shame to only have one in the story, they seemed to do everything better as a team. While one had his cock up her pussy, the other could be fucking her mouth. Or would between her tits be steamier? So maybe two Marines? Or do you think three would be better?"

I'm shrieking and laughing as he flips me over his knee and raises my skirt. The crack of his palm against my ass sounds worse than the sting that follows. It's followed in quick succession by three more. My laughter fades to moans as my clit bounces hard against his muscled thigh. Two more and I'm gushing with need. It truly doesn't hurt, not the way Aiden is doing it, anyway. I wiggle, trying to get better friction so I can cum before he calms down, but he clamps his other leg against mine, holding me in place. He swats my rear twice more, lighter and higher up. Then he stops. I wait, my head and arms dangling, "Aiden? Everything okay up there?"

"I'm trying to decide your real punishment for teasing me like that. I'm leaning towards not letting you cum until after we get back from dinner."

I moan, clenching my thighs, hoping it might be enough to finish what he started. It's not, and he pulls me upright before I can try anything else. "Seriously, Rosey, did they have to be Marines? You couldn't have gone with the Army?"

"I go with what works, Commander McBride." I glance at the clock, "I'll change so we can go eat."

He holds me tight on his lap, "No. You're going just as you are."

"But, Aiden! I'm really wet. I need panties." I grimace.

"Perhaps one of your Marines can lend you something. Just as you are, Rosebud. Maybe wet thighs will teach you to behave in the future. I suggest you keep your legs together." He's grinning at my pout.

I kiss him thoroughly, "Thank you for going there for me, despite the fact that I'm now wet and throbbing with need."

"You do suffer for your art, Rose. I hope your readers appreciate it."

We go to dinner and he *is* careful to walk close behind me as we move to and from the table. I can barely concentrate on what I'm eating, though. Partly because I'm still wound up with no orgasm in sight, but also because Aiden is beautiful when he gets all possessive and bossy. His eyes blaze and his lips get this hard edge that feels glorious when he kisses me. He reins it in 99.9% of the time, so the rare glimpses I catch where his control slips are worth the wait.

We don't make it upstairs when we get home. No sooner are we clear of the front door then he's lifting me up and pinning me against the wall in the entryway. He frees his cock and pulls me down onto it, sliding balls deep in that single motion. His mouth grinds against mine as his hips piston, pushing his cock deeper into me than I would have thought possible. A few more thrusts and we're both cumming hard. His seed is leaking down my thighs when he finally turns and carries me upstairs, his cock still pulsing within me.

His cock slides free when he sets me down on my feet by the bed. He pulls my skirt back up and rubs his hand gently over my pussy through our mingled cum. "Mine, Rose. This pussy, you, never going to let you go."

"You won't get the chance, I'd have to let go first." I can be just as fierce when I'm protecting what I love.

He helps me off with my dress, and while normally I would shower, there's something special about tonight. I think we both need to feel each other on our skin. I pull him down on top of me and this time we make love slowly and completely. Dotting the i's and crossing all the t's. I bite his earlobe gently, then suck it hard. He spends five minutes kissing the inner curve of my hip. The release that rolls in on waves is no less intense for having built up more slowly.

I'm splayed out on Aiden's chest, his hands cupping my ass when I finally manage to ask, "So… yes or no to spanking in the future?"

He's quiet for a long minute, "A conditional maybe. First condition, you take *all* your punishment like a good girl."

God, I think I just came again. Aiden's idea of punishment is really not the kind that makes me sorry. And when he says 'good girl' like that? I want to suck him dry right then and there.

"Next, it's not a routine thing. Stop pouting, Mrs. McBride."

"How do you know I'm pouting?" I am so pouting.

"I can feel it. And finally, we're not doing that again while you're pregnant."

Aiden

Rose stills on top of me, "You know?"

"I'm guessing," I admit. "Were you going to tell me soon?"

"I don't actually know for sure. I bought a test this afternoon but our um, evening went a little longer than anticipated. Not that I'm complaining."

"So your research was satisfactory?"

"Very. I'll be sure to thank you in the dedication."

I groan. She always puts something corny and embarrassing in there and doesn't let me see it until the book is published. I usually get a call from Linda that leads with cackling. That's how I know the book's gone live.

Rose braces her arms on my chest, resting her chin on her hands, "You haven't said how you feel about the yet-to-be-confirmed baby…"

"I have mixed feelings," I admit but regret it when I see anxiety sweep across her eyes before settling into a frown. "Relax, Rose. We've already talked about this. I'm still in agreement on having kids. It's not about wanting it, but I don't want to see you in pain or even uncomfortable. It's something I have no control over and very little influence. I don't much care for that. But I'll do whatever I can to protect you. You're going to be ready to kill me long before the third trimester."

She starts to say something but I stop her with a finger to her lips, "But seeing you get round with our child, to know that it was my cock flooding your pussy with cum that made it happen? That's plenty of compensation for not being in complete control. As long as you promise not to overdo it, take all your vitamins, and let me pamper you."

"Aiden, you're absolutely huggable, you know that?"

"I was going for sensitive alpha male. Maybe I need to be bossier?" I ask as I flip us over and imprison her delicate wrists in my left hand. I use my free hand to tease and tickle her until she's laughing and crying 'uncle'. Then I settle between her thighs and kiss her breathless. "Love you, Rosebud."

"Darla and I both adore you," she whispers back, which makes me laugh.

Hi there! I hope you enjoyed reading Rose and Aiden's story? The number one question I get asked by readers is where is Ing and Justin's? I'm so excited to be able to share that Provoked is finally available! And of course, Rose makes an appearance as her BFF confronts her own confused emotions.

OTHER BOOKS

When Busted was first published, I also got quite a few requests for more of Darla's debut novel Deal with the Devil. So I wrote it... and it got sillier and more crazy the farther I went with it. Naturally, it's now a firm fan favorite! John just may steal your heart — you've been warned...

Resisting Daphne

Acceptable Limits

Finding Alexei

Chasing Burke

Braving Cash

Her Christmas Beast

Her Billionaire Beast

Her Reclusive Beast (coming soon!)

If you like steamy short reads, also check out:

Tough Guys Read Romance

Truly Devious Matchmakers

The Mountain Men of SEAL Team Delta Tango

Thanks for Reading!

If you loved this story and can take a minute to leave a review, you will help other readers find it!

And to find out what's next or whatever other crazy idea has entered my head, come join my newsletter!

ABOUT OLIVIA SINCLAIR

I write steamy romance that's safe, funny, and totally over the top. My heroes are always alpha males because the stronger they are, the harder they fall. Luckily the smart, sassy heroines know how to catch them and make everything better!

I never get tired of believing that love can show up unexpectedly and with determination. That it can find you anywhere, even curled up on the couch, in your jammies, while eating ice cream and binging romance novels. Then a knock on the door reveals your gorgeous new neighbor that you didn't even know had moved in... or maybe it's that hot friend of your dad's you only know through photos...

Possibly the HEAs come easier because my home and office are in a romantic clearing of giant evergreens in the Pacific Northwest. Think Snow White without the Dwarves. But I do have a bounty of wild animals that come to visit. There's even a resident nuthatch that talks to itself (constantly)! And there are currently seven chickens in the henhouse...

You can find me and my books along with lots of fun extras on my website: https://oliviasinclairbooks.com or email me directly at oliviasinclairbooks@gmail.com. I love to know who my readers are and what you love to see in a good story!